LOOK FOR ME

BOOKS BY JAN THOMPSON

Protector Sweethearts (6 Books)
JanThompson.com/protector

Defender Sweethearts (6 Books)
JanThompson.com/defender

Binary Hackers (4 Books)
JanThompson.com/binary

Seaside Chapel (6 Books)
JanThompson.com/seaside

Savannah Sweethearts (11 Books)
JanThompson.com/savannah

Vacation Sweethearts (8 Books)
JanThompson.com/vacation

Keep up with Jan Thompson's book news:
JanThompson.com/newsletter

LOOK FOR ME

VACATION SWEETHEARTS BOOK 4

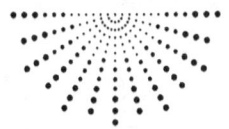

JAN THOMPSON

GEORGIA
PRESS

LOOK FOR ME (VACATION SWEETHEARTS BOOK 4)

Copyright © 2020 Jan Edttii Lim Thompson

Author Website: JanThompson.com
Book News: JanThompson.com/newsletter
Published by Georgia Press LLC

Scripture taken from the New King James Version®. Copyright © 1982 by Thomas Nelson. Used by permission. All rights reserved.
The lyrics for the "This is My Father's World" hymn penned by Maltbie D. Babcock in the late 19th century are in the public domain.

Cover Design: Deranged Doctor Design

eBook ISBN 978-1-944188-56-6
Paperback ISBN 978-1-944188-57-3

To my Lord and Savior, Jesus Christ, who died on the cross to save me from my sins and rose again from the grave to give me eternal life in heaven.

For God so loved the world that He gave His only begotten Son, that whoever believes in Him should not perish but have everlasting life.
—John 3:16

READ THE VACATION
SWEETHEARTS PREQUEL
FOR FREE

When art gallery archivist Sheryl Breckenridge tries to get world-famous sculptor Winton Pace to display his artwork at Simon's Gallery, she doesn't expect him to fall in love with her. Will she reciprocate in this friends-to-more romance?

Read *Time for Me* (A Vacation Sweethearts Prequel) for FREE at the link below. This story starts thirteen months before *Smile for Me* (Vacation Sweethearts Book 1).

Download the FREE prequel here:
JanThompson.com/time-free

Sign up for Jan Thompson's mailing list to keep up with her book news. She writes Christian beach romance, romantic suspense, and suspense thrillers.

Subscribe to Jan's book news:
JanThompson.com/newsletter

ABOUT LOOK FOR ME (VACATION SWEETHEARTS BOOK 4)

She needs a champion.
Just not him.

Four years after his girlfriend ghosted him, Martin MacFarland finds her in south Florida—abused, pregnant with her second child, and in danger.

Martin wants to be there for her, but she can't give him a second chance.

Remember the MacFarlands in *Smile for Me* (Vacation Sweethearts Book 1)? *Look for Me* is the story of Tina's brother, Martin. We visit the southern coast of Florida, where Martin MacFarland goes to find his long-lost ex-girlfriend.

This Christian beach town romance novel with a side of suspense has clean language while dealing with the difficulties of past sins, single motherhood, second chances, redemption, and the mercy of God.

SHE NEEDS A CHAMPION...

A single mother on the run, Corinne Anderson has made many mistakes since she broke up with Martin MacFarland four years ago. Each mistake compounds on the other problems in her life.

Down and out, Corinne and her three-year-old daughter end up in the small beach town of Key Largo, hiding from the criminals looking for them. When their witness protection cover is blown, Corinne needs all the help she can get to stay safe.

As long as it's not from Martin.

ANYONE BUT HIM...

After his father gives him half the ownership of the MacMuscles Classic Car Restoration business in Savannah, Georgia, Martin MacFarland is convinced that he is ready to settle down and start a family. Unfortunately for him, the only woman he ever loved has vanished without a trace.

After his private investigator tracks her down, Martin drives to Key Largo, praying that Corinne will forgive him for what he did before he became a Christian, and hoping she might consider starting over with him.

Well, she can't. And she won't tell him why either.

YET HE WON'T LEAVE...

As Martin gets closer to finding out what Corinne is up to or hiding from, will he fall into the same fire that has burned Corinne so many times? Will his love survive the flames?

Look for Me is the fourth novel in *USA Today* Bestselling author Jan Thompson's **Vacation Sweethearts** Christian travel romance series celebrating the immeasurable grace and undeserved mercy of God through Jesus Christ. These standalone novels are a spin-off of her **Savannah Sweethearts** beach romance series. Some of the novels in **Vacation Sweethearts** are also a prelude to the **Protector Sweethearts** Christian romantic suspense series.

Look for Me (Vacation Sweethearts Book 4):
JanThompson.com/look

Vacation Sweethearts:
JanThompson.com/vacation

Subscribe to Jan's Mailing List for Book News:
JanThompson.com/newsletter

LOOK FOR ME

CHAPTER ONE

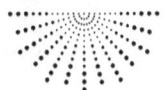

*M*artin MacFarland parked his bright tangerine 1966 Shelby GT350 in the last spot by the curb. He lifted his sunglasses to take a clearer look across the small street.

On a sidewalk bench in front of the Key Largo Chocolate Shop, a woman wearing a bright orange apron—that matched the colors of the sign above the windows behind her—was eating her sandwich the way his ex-girlfriend would—all around the edges first. Martin remembered teasing her about her eccentricities when they had both worked at his sister's pottery studio, she as the office manager and he as his sister's personal assistant.

Could that be Corinne Anderson?

Except for her long hair—in a new honey blonde color and tied back in a ponytail—she didn't look much different from the last time Martin had seen her two days after his sister's wedding four years before.

Had it been that long?

The August sunshine swept across the treeless Florida road, casting a bright spotlight on the woman seated on the bench. The more Martin stared, the more confident he was that she was Corinne.

I should never have let her go.

He hadn't forgotten her after she ghosted him as soon as they broke up four years ago, but it wasn't until he'd had a string of failed relationships for the next three years that he realized what he had missed.

Now that he was an income-producing co-owner of MacMuscles Classic Car Restoration, he could afford to settle down—with the right woman.

His sister Tina reminded him that Corinne hadn't shown signs of being a Christian when she walked out of his life. Today, she might still be unsaved. If so, her worldview would be different from Martin's. He had to keep in mind who would raise his future children.

Would the mother of his kids be willing to take

them to a Christian church if she didn't believe in God or Jesus Christ?

Nonetheless, Martin had to find Corinne. Whether she was a believer or not, Martin wanted to ask her forgiveness for stringing her along and then trying to marry her when he felt guilty about their intimate relationship.

It had taken Martin one more year to track her down, with most of the work done by his private investigator friend, Ming Wei, who had connections all over North America.

Corinne Anderson was Dinah Miller now, but the records showed she wasn't married.

The reason she was living under an assumed name was anybody's guess. Why did she change her name? Why was she hiding from the world?

And from me, perhaps?

Well, Martin figured she must not be in too much danger—because she only ran as far away as Key Largo, Florida.

He could make the drive in eight hours if he drove straight through—nine, if he stopped to refill the gas tank and get food.

No, he didn't have to ask Ming for permission— even though Ming had specifically told him that he didn't have more information beyond the chocolate shop. The private investigator was working on something, but he wouldn't know what to tell Martin until Monday.

Monday!

After a restless four or five hours of sleep, Martin was wide awake at two o'clock on Thursday morning. Staring at the ceiling, he made a snap decision to go. He hurriedly packed up a small overnight bag, and he was on the road in thirty minutes, reaching Key Largo at 11:30 a.m., stopping at a fast food drive through along the way.

Fifteen minutes later, there she was. On the bench, under the sun.

As clear as day, that was Corinne.

Martin unbuckled his safety belt, but didn't leave the driver's seat. He drank the remaining lukewarm coffee from a late breakfast as his eyes fixed upon Corinne, aka Dinah, who had finished her lunch.

Martin rolled down his window. The blast of hot Florida air slapped away the cool air inside his car. It must be at least ninety degrees.

It was then that it felt odd to Martin that Corinne was wearing such oversized long-sleeved shirt and baggy pants.

As long as Martin had known her, she was the spaghetti-strap type of girl, going to work at Tina's office in sleeveless blouses whenever she could, even if the air-conditioner was on full blast in the pottery studio.

However, four years later in subtropical Florida —with a late summer even hotter than coastal Georgia—Corinne was wearing such shapeless clothes. Why?

He wanted a closer look.

Martin watched her enter the chocolate shop. He rolled up his window. Time to confront her, to see if she still remembered him—or cared to remember him.

How do I approach her?

Martin prayed to God for wisdom. He had been saved for only four years and his prayers were not yet as strong or clear as his sister's or his brother-in-law's, who was now the assistant pastor at a church in metro Atlanta.

However, Pastor Flores from Martin's own church said that God would hear the prayers of his heart even if he couldn't form the words. As he learned to pray more, he would have more words to pray.

Martin willed his heart to speak to God, though he could not come up with anything concrete or specific. Perhaps the coffee had spiked his system to the point of making him jittery. Perhaps the drive from Savannah had sapped his strength. Whatever it was, he couldn't find the words.

Finally, he bleated a weak, "Read my heart, Lord Jesus."

It would have to do. Otherwise he might as well go home.

His only purpose of coming down to this small beach town was to get a glimpse of the only woman he truly loved.

Now he must talk to her, to see if she was real, that she wasn't a doppelgänger. To see if she still remembered him. If there was still any hope for them.

And if she had met Jesus since their sad parting.

No doubt it would be a difficult conversation. Their breakup had been anything but sweet. On the day before Tina's wedding, Martin had accepted Jesus Christ as his personal Lord and Savior, thereby making him a brand-new man who wouldn't sleep with Corinne any more until their wedding night.

"I don't want to marry you!" Those were her last words as she threw his apartment keys at him—leaving a small scar on his cheek—and walked out into the streets of Savannah in the pouring evening rain.

The next day, she quit her job at Tina's Turn Pottery Studio, moved out of her house, sold her car, changed her phone number, cut off all contacts with her friends and relatives, and disappeared from Martin's world.

Until now.

CHAPTER TWO

"*T*hat was a quick lunch, Dinah." Sandra Preston, the chocolate shop owner, was washing a giant copper bowl in the sink when Corinne walked past by her.

"Fifteen minutes. Plenty of time to eat a sandwich. Besides, I have to make up for the doctor's visit yesterday." Corinne washed her hands at another sink.

"Yes. How's your little girl?"

"She's okay now. All the red spots are subsiding. She's learning not to scratch."

"That's hard for a three-year-old, but I was never allergic to ants."

"It's not an allergy per se. She just had a reaction because there were too many bites."

"Falling on an anthill will do that to you."

"I know." There was nothing Corinne could do. She could not afford daycare, and preschool was closed for the summer.

All she could do was rely on the octogenarian Wanda Lewis—known to everyone at church as Wanda—to babysit Dahlia while she worked all day here and then as a server on weekends at a local bar. Wanda had poor eyesight and even poorer hearing. Dahlia would sneak out to play in the backyard alone. It was fenced in, but the ants were already inside the yard.

Corinne remembered panicking when Wanda called her yesterday, saying that Dahlia was screaming for help in the backyard. Her co-worker Hardin gave Corinne a ride back to the house and took them to urgent care.

And paid for it out of his pocket and the generosity of his heart. Corinne prayed that the pastry chef would not ask for something she could not give in return.

She felt bad that, without any health insurance, she would have to rely on the mercy of others.

Minimum wage and never rising up, she couldn't even afford her own car. Every penny she earned went to feed her daughter and pay for the one bedroom she rented from Wanda Lewis, whose sister used to live with her before she had to move to a nursing home.

Corinne had thought about getting a job at the Walmart in Homestead across the causeway, but it was a forty-five minute drive each way. Not having a car didn't help.

She had also found out about retail jobs at a couple of gift shops in Islamorada, half an hour south of here—but again, no car, no help.

Maybe she could ask Sandra for forty hours and healthcare benefits. However, this was probably a bad time. The widowed owner of the establishment seemed busy right now.

Really, there was no good time. Key Largo was a tourist stop, and this chocolate shop was famous for its chocolate barks and pralines.

Corinne looked for a clean kitchen towel to hand over to Sandra, who thanked her for it. "Want me to help you put that away?"

"No. You better get up front," Sandra said. "Erika hasn't come back from her dental appointment."

"Oh. I'm sorry." Corinne hurried for the door leading out to the old store.

Surrounded by red brick walls, the Key Largo Chocolate Shop was basically an open space with old kitchen tables and cabinets filled with chocolate, fudge, brownies, truffles, petits fours, you name it. Oh yes, and ice cream.

Corinne reached the counter, where a line was forming. She opened the next cash register. "May I help the next person?"

The tourist was laden with several cameras, some with telephoto lenses, hanging every which way off his neck. He was sweating heavily.

Corinne handed him a wad of paper napkins. The man thanked her in a thick accent, and began to wipe his forehead—lobster-red and flushed with sweat.

Corinne regretted helping him as soon as he did that. The napkin fell apart on his face. Bits and pieces of paper were stuck to his forehead and cheeks.

Oh, no.

She didn't know what to say. She looked around, found a roll of paper towels, and tore off a few sheets for him. The man thanked her again.

That helped some.

Corinne tried not to look at him. She rang up his five boxes of double chocolate fudge with extra maple syrup and cut cherries on top. He swiped his card, and waddled out of the store with the shopping bag.

Anyone who worked in this store had trained to

work at all the stations, even helping Hardin to make their signature items. That way, if someone called in sick, another person could fill in, and the shop would continue to function.

Usually, Corinne was at the back, stirring melted chocolate or making brownies and fudge and other sweet things she had no cravings for. Her entire life, she had never experienced any sweet tooth. She didn't know whether it was genetic or not, since her mother had passed away many years ago. She never knew her father, and didn't know if she inherited a sweet tooth—or for that matter, any medical problem, from him either.

Perhaps it wasn't ironic that she was a single mother now too.

But yeah, no sweet tooth.

With Erika late for work, Corinne had to fill in wherever Sandra put her today. Out front, Corinne had to smile to the customers and be as polite as she could.

Back in Savannah, when she still had a job that provided her with 401K and health insurance, she was an office manager at a pottery studio. Sure, there were customers coming and going—buying pottery or taking classes—but for the most part, Corinne didn't have to greet anyone with a smile on her face.

Especially when her entire body ached all over.

She shouldn't have taken that short cut last night through the alley—

The cabinets rattled as a stampede of kids stormed in. They looked like they were from the nearby camp. Corinne wished she could afford to send Dahlia to camp someday.

The kids oohed and aahed and licked their lips as their noses and palms pressed against the clear glass panel separating them from the ice cream bar.

From the corner of Corinne's eye, she spotted Erika rushing in, tying up her apron and then putting on a pair of gloves. The children all spoke at once. Their chaperone tried to calm them down.

Must be nice to be so young and carefree.

Corinne bagged and checked out a dozen customers before she could go lean against something or sit down to rest her sore feet. She had bought the tennis shoes from Walmart about a year ago, and had worn down the inside sole. She lined it with a new insole only yesterday, but it might not be enough.

Every night, she'd go home with sore feet and aching joints from half an hour of walking. That was why she had taken the short cut last night.

Bad move.

Thank God that a couple of homeless men had

wandered into the alley to dumpster dive. They scared off her attackers, but not before Corinne saw their faces.

They were the same attackers from two months before, although that was on another street several blocks away. Some passersby stopped the attack and called the police. Corinne ended up in the hospital, and was released the next day before she contacted her FBI handler.

A week later, the police found her attacker dead, beaten to a pulp.

Corinne didn't believe her FBI handler had sent someone to mete out justice for her. She was more apt to think it was Flavian.

It had to be.

Flavian Bailey was her ex-boyfriend in Nevada. Corinne had refused to remember him for two years, but could he have found her, even though she changed her name from Gail to Dinah?

Flavian was the reason she had to go into the United States Federal Witness Protection Program with her daughter. Rarely a violent man—he had others do his dirty work for him—Flavian lost it when he discovered that his favorite girl turned out to be an FBI informant.

Still, Flavian could never hurt Corinne.

He would even defend her.

However, the FBI wouldn't take any chances. Corinne's handler terminated her spying activities, and removed her from Las Vegas. Mother and child ended up in a safe house before they were whisked away by Federal Marshals who deposited them in Key Largo, at the house of one Wanda Preston.

WITSEC or not, this safe haven hadn't prevented her from being raped by some drunken stranger, who had evidently paid for his life.

She should leave Florida altogether. But she had no money to go far, and wouldn't dream of hitchhiking with a three-year-old in tow.

To be honest, Corinne was tired of running.

The door chimes jingled and jangled incessantly. Every now and then a whoosh of the afternoon heat pulsated into the shop. The ceiling fan spun quietly above, and the air-conditioning was at full blast, but all that wasn't going to help much if the door to the hot Florida sun kept opening and closing.

However, such a thing was typical in June. After all, all the beach towns along the Florida Keys, from Key Largo to Key West, were huge tourist hangouts. People came here from all over the world, practically all year round. With school out for the summer in the United States, domestic tourists also flocked to the area. About the only time the chocolate shop had no customers was hurricane season.

Otherwise, Key Largo was filled with northern snow birds in winter, students during spring breaks, homeschoolers in the off-seasons, and people on vacation year round. They came to see the ocean, do some diving and deep-sea fishing, and dine on fresh sea food.

And maybe eat some homemade chocolate too.

"There you go." Corinne handed another bag of yummies to the next customer. She was one of the many indecisive tourists who bought a little of everything. They sold sampler boxes up on the shelves, but most people wanted to pick their own samples.

She scanned the store to see how many customers there were currently. A few walked out without buying anything. That was highly unusual, but it happened.

The door chimed again, and Corinne glanced that way—

No. It can't be.

Corinne felt lightheaded.

Her knees buckled.

Then she felt nothing.

CHAPTER THREE

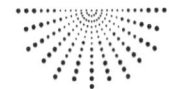

"*D*inah? Dinah?"

Faintly, distorted and indistinct as though in a tunnel, the voices kept repeating the name.

Who is Dinah?

Whoever you are, Dinah, you better respond!

Corinne tried to open her eyes, but her vision was fuzzy—as though she was waking up from sleep.

What's going on? Why did I...

"Let's carry her to the back office. We have customers here." Sandra's voice was a mix of concern and...regret?

"Is she pregnant?" Erika's voice.

"Should we call 911?" Hardin, oh Hardin.

"No, no. I'm fine." *Most definitely, do not call 911.*

That would cost money. Without insurance, Corinne could not afford it.

"I don't want to be a burden to anyone," she found herself saying.

She couldn't get up.

Her eyes finally opened. Someone was staring down directly at her.

"Are you all right?" Sandra asked.

"Please don't fire me. I need this job. I'll...I'll get back to work."

"You'll do no such thing," Sandra said. "I'm giving you the rest of the day off."

"Maybe it was too hot outside. I just need some cold water." Corinne struggled to sit up. She held her head.

What happened?

"Hardin can drive you home," Sandra said. "You should see the doctor ASAP. I don't want you passing out again."

Corinne nodded even though she knew she wasn't going to follow through.

Doctors cost money. She had to save every dime to feed herself and her daughter.

I won't let Dahlia down like everybody else has let me down.

"Where's Hardin?" Sandra asked.

"I'll take her home," a deep voice said.

Martin MacFarland.

I'm dreaming.

Corinne dared not look in the direction of the voice. She pulled her shirt across her belly to cover up her baby bump.

"Who are you?" Sandra said to the voice from Corinne's past.

"I'm an old friend. She knows me. I'll take her home."

Still sitting on the floor, Corinne didn't want to look at him. At the back of her mind, she should have expected that somehow she would have to face reality one way or another at some point in her life.

Though not this soon, God. Not this soon.

Corinne breathed in and out. Steeled herself as best she could, and rose to her feet—with the help of many hands. They moved her away from the main aisle behind the counter toward the back of the store. Sandra gave her a cup of cold water. Then she went back to work, leaving Corinne sitting on a chair by the wall.

She lifted her chin, and there he was.

I wasn't dreaming. It's really him.

Martin MacFarland looked older. His haircut

19

was shorter now. Neater and tidier. He wore a Hawaiian shirt with faded geometric patterns. Scruffy deck shoes. Canvas, probably. His favorite.

He didn't have a band on his ring finger.

Corinne didn't know why her thought went to that, but it made all the difference in the world.

If he were married, she would not want to accept his help to get her home.

Then again, he had found her. It had to be on purpose. What if he didn't wear his wedding ring on purpose?

Well, okay.

Either way, she had to say *no*.

There was no way she would want him to go near her ramshackle house. He would see Dahlia. Ask questions. Judge her with his Christian faith.

Now I'm a Christian too, although only for under a year.

"Y-you're...pregnant?" Martin blurted.

Corinne didn't reply, as if talking to him would make things more difficult for both of them.

"Leave. Please leave." It was curt, but she didn't want Martin to get any idea.

"I came here to ask you to forgive me," Martin said. "You're pregnant."

Corinne could imagine the shock on Martin's face.

Sometimes in the dark of night, she had thought of him and wondered what they would say if they saw each other again. One of the things she thought she should do was to ask for his forgiveness.

But he got to it first.

"If you want me to leave, I'll leave." Martin kept his voice down.

"Go," Corinne said, trying not to cry.

Get out of my life and don't come back.

Martin nodded, just as Hardin showed up, all flustered.

"Dinah, you okay?" He blurted.

"Could you take me home, please?" Corinne asked.

"Of course. Let's go." Hardin reached for Corinne's hand and helped her to her feet.

Corinne walked by Martin, refusing to look at him at all.

She had no idea what Martin thought about that, but she wanted to send a clear signal to him that whatever they had in the past was long gone and never to be rekindled.

It was gone.

And so were the best days of her life.

Stunned, Martin stayed rooted to the spot, watching Corinne leave with some guy, who seemed to be another worker at the store. He tried to recall his name. Earlier, the older woman had asked for some guy to take Corinne home. This must be the dude.

Tell me it's not his shirt that Corinne was wearing.

Worse yet, tell me she's not carrying his baby.

He wondered if he should follow them.

I'm not a stalker.

"Sir, please," someone said to him. "Customers are not supposed to be on this side."

"Ah. Sorry. I was trying to help Corinne..." Martin backed away toward the aisle that led to the front of the store.

"Who?"

"Dinah. Must've gotten her mixed up with someone else." He had forgotten that she was living under an alias.

"Don't worry about it. It's probably just the heat, like she said. I told her not to sit outside in the sun."

"She does like the sunshine."

The girl gave Martin an odd look. "You know her? How?"

"We're old friends. Could you tell me when she works?"

"We don't give out employee hours."

"Okay. How early are you open in the morning?"

The woman pointed to the sign on the glass windows. The words and hours were printed in reverse.

"Thank you." Martin wanted to be on good terms with the people who work here. He didn't want anyone to get in his way of another meeting with Corinne.

"What's good in here?" He asked.

"Everything is good." She pointed to chunks of fudge. "Would you like some samples to help you decide?"

Martin salivated at the array of choices. He picked all dark chocolate, but in at least five different flavors. Then he felt bad he couldn't make up his mind. So he bought a quarter pound of each of the five fudge types.

Across the street, he ate half of them before he put his car in gear.

That was when he spotted Hardin at the gas station next to where he parked. Hardin was getting gas for his vehicle. Inside the car was a passenger who looked like Corinne from the back.

She must have her window rolled down, because Hardin was talking in an animated fashion.

Something pulled at Martin's heart.

He put on his safety belt, and cranked up his Shelby.

CHAPTER FOUR

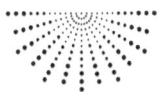

*T*he last person Corinne expected to see in Key Largo was Martin MacFarland. Even though they were on the same Atlantic Coast, Corinne had a new life now. For all practical purposes, Martin was dead to her.

She felt her baby kick.

Flavian's baby.

It wasn't the baby's fault, Corinne kept telling herself.

Corinne stopped at the edge of the patch of grass and looked out to sea. She breathed in the afternoon air, hot and swirling around her. It wasn't cooled down yet by the breeze from the Atlantic Ocean.

She had asked Hardin to drop her off by the

roadside several blocks away so that she could clear her head as she walked home the rest of the way. It was daylight, and she was in open space.

Corinne felt safe.

She hadn't been assaulted in two months.

Going in the opposite direction now, she walked down a small lane leading to the public beach access. She crossed the boardwalk, took off her shoes, and stepped on the soft sand. The sand felt summery hot as she had expected on this June afternoon, but Corinne didn't want to wear her shoes and get sand in them.

Corinne walked along the ocean's edge, cooling down her feet as she sloshed her way along the beach. Praying, thinking, praying, mulling over her life.

When she didn't get a ride home from Erika or Hardin, this was her usual walking route to and from work, day in and day out, rain or shine—every day except Sunday when Pete from church gave them a ride to the morning service.

One Sunday afternoon, after a potluck lunch at a church member's house, Corinne heard the salvation message. That evening, she asked Wanda what that was all about.

Wanda explained what Jesus had done for Corinne on the cross of Calvary, how He carried

Corinne's sins on His shoulders, and sacrificed Himself to set her free from the guilt and shame of her sins.

Weeping on Wanda's shoulder, Corinne saw the intensity of God's love for her.

That night, Corinne accepted Jesus as her personal Lord and Savior. The next morning, she woke up to the surprise of her life.

The weight of all her life's burdens were gone from her shoulders.

Life was still hard, but now she had hope in Christ.

She still had to face the difficulties of her life as it was, but she no longer felt the heavy weight and the stress of that burden pressing down on her shoulders.

She was free.

Just like what Wanda said God would do for her.

Therefore if the Son makes you free, you shall be free indeed.

For the next few weeks after her salvation, Corinne joined a Bible study with the other mothers in her preschool group. She memorized that verse from John 8:36, along with several other verses for new believers in Christ.

Still, it would be a couple of months later at the Christmas Eve service when it all sank in for her. The entire weight of her sins was still gone. "Jesus had paid it all, and carried it all."

That was the most peaceful Christmas in her entire life.

I still can't believe that You saved me, Lord.

She smiled to no one on the open space. Somewhere along the shoreline, visitors here and there played at the water's edge. Local residents knew better than to come out here at two o'clock in the afternoon.

Air conditioning would be nice about now.

Then again, this was Key Largo. If she wanted to live here, she'd have to get used to how warm it was going to be all year round.

This wasn't like Savannah...

Oh, she wished she hadn't thought of Savannah. That always brought back memories of a past she wished she could forget forever, memories like...

Martin.

Back at the chocolate shop, he had clearly stated his case. He had a reason for tracking her down.

I came here to ask you to forgive me.

After four years.

Shouldn't it go both ways?

Corinne didn't want to know. In fact, she decided there and then to call in sick the next day. It would be a lie, but she could not face Martin.

Not with all these problems swirling around her.

Why did God bring him back into my life?

She wondered if it was to give her a chance to say goodbye once and for all?

That couldn't possibly happen.

She could not see Martin again. By showing up at her workplace, he had already caused a lot of problems for her.

Everyone there knew her as Dinah Miller, not Corinne Anderson. It had all happened before she became a Christian. However, after she accepted Jesus, she still needed the money to pay rent and could not tell her employer the whole truth.

Besides, Dinah Miller was her legal name now, thanks to WITSEC.

Corinne blinked away bitter tears. "Lord Jesus, why do I have so many problems?"

And then this pregnancy...

Why is my life so messed up?

She stared at the saltwater around her feet. The ocean was loud, the wind was picking up.

How easy it would be to walk into the ocean and never return to shore!

Yet, Dahlia needed her. There was no way Wanda, with her arthritis and a host of other aging problems, would be able to raise a child not her own.

Corinne backed away from the ocean, walked back across the sand and over the boardwalk. She found a public faucet, washed her feet there, and wiped them dry with a small hand towel she carried with her in her shopping tote.

Then she crossed the two-way street and found the small beach road between a row of houses.

Four more blocks and she'd be home.

Home?

This is not home. It's only a temporary hiding place.

The sidewalk was empty and quiet.

Too quiet.

Where were all the tourists and residents?

The condominiums, beach, and ocean were all behind her now. She was heading toward a residential area, where Wanda lived.

Her feet kept walking, but she regretted now that she hadn't let Hardin drive her home.

Couldn't she have walked on the beach another day?

Every now and then a vehicle passed by her. She felt safer already. Then she heard a car slow down.

"You okay?"

Corinne closed her eyes and drew a deep breath.

I knew it.

She turned toward the voice. Two men in a car. "Hi Slam, Slime."

They weren't twins, but they were certainly brothers in arms. They had worked for Flavian for many years.

"We're changing our nicknames." Slime laughed from the passenger side. "You need a ride home?"

"How did you find me?" Corinne stood rooted at the sidewalk.

Slime glanced at Slam, as if wondering whether to say anything.

"You can tell me the truth." Corinne tried to remain calm.

Slime nodded. "When Flavian found out what happened to you two months ago, they sent us here."

"You still didn't explain how you found me."

"The same way we knew that jerk—no rest for his soul—attacked you."

Slam leaned over from the driver's side. "You don't have to keep the baby, you know, on account that the father is deceased."

"Did you... Were you the ones..." Corinne's jaw dropped.

"We plead the fifth." Slam looked mighty proud of himself.

"We've been watching over you all this time," the other said.

"All this time? Like how?" Corinne's legs wobbled.

"WITSEC is overrated." Slam laughed.

"We've been watching over your house," Slime added. "Flavian doesn't want his baby girl hurt."

It hit Corinne like a rock. "You know where I live."

"Uh-huh. FBI is like a leaky sieve." Slam laughed again.

Now Corinne regretted contacting her FBI handler. Flavian knew where she was. Then again, why hadn't he come after her? "Where's Flavian?"

Slime shrugged. "He doesn't tell us. Our job is to keep you safe. So you want a ride home or not?"

Corinne had told herself never to get into any

vehicle owned or sent by Flavian. "No, thanks. I need to walk."

"Like I said, we know where you live," Slime reminded her. "We've been taking turns sleeping in the car for two months."

"Thank you. That's very kind of you." What else could Corinne say. "I'll still walk."

"You want us to follow you?" Slim asked.

"We better," Slime said. "Or we'll never hear the end of it from Flavian if she's attacked again."

Corinne winced. She did not want to recall the episode. Maybe she should let them escort her home. Then again, who was to say these two weren't lying to her about knowing where she lived.

I can't take any chances.

She made an about turn and walked back into town. She didn't know who to call. Hardin was no match for these two guys. Martin would be, but she had no idea how to contact him.

What about Erika? She seemed to know martial arts.

A loud car honk startled her. She turned to look.

An SUV pulled up at the curb. The passenger window rolled down.

And out of the car, Corinne heard Erika's voice. "Sorry I'm late!"

What a relief! Corinne nearly cried. She waved to the two men in the car nearby, and made a beeline for the passenger side.

She climbed in and locked the door. "Thank you, Erika. I thought you were working."

"Hardin went back to work so I asked him how you were doing. When I found out he dropped you off by the side of the road, I nearly punched him."

"You didn't." Corinne laughed nervously.

Erika glanced in her rearview mirror, and then eased into the light traffic. "So who are those two men back there?"

"Old friends from the past."

"They giving you any trouble?"

Corinne shook her head.

Not yet.

"You must be tired, but we need to drive around a bit so that those men don't follow us," Erika suggested.

"Yeah? Okay. I'm not expected home for a few more hours anyway."

"Tell me about that man who was in the store earlier—the one who made you swoon." Erika chuckled.

"I didn't *swoon*. I felt lightheaded, is all."

"Could've fooled me. Is he the boyfriend you left behind somewhere out there?"

"Prying, aren't you?" Corinne knew she could trust Erika, but now wasn't the time to ask about Martin.

She was referring to Martin, wasn't she?

The boyfriend I left behind.

"Well, it seems that he has caught up to me." Corinne looked out the window and said no more.

CHAPTER FIVE

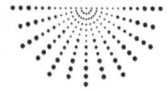

"Mommy! Mommy!" Dahlia burst out of the front door of the small weather-worn house, ran down the stone path in her bare feet, and lifted her arms high in the air.

Corinne closed the small gate behind her, and scooped up her daughter in her arms. "Sweetheart, have you been a good girl today?"

Dahlia nodded. "I good."

Corinne glanced behind her, spotting Erika driving away.

"Let's see your arms." Corinne inspected her daughter's arms. Up and down her arms, the red welts and bite marks were subsiding.

Thank God they look better now.

"Itchy, Mommy." Tears pooled in Dahlia's eyes.

"I know, baby. I know." Corinne hugged her daughter tightly.

"Aunt V helped me put mack-sin."

Medicine. "Good. Did you thank her?"

"Yes, Mommy."

Corinne carried Dahlia to the door, where Wanda stood with her walking stick. "Thank you, Wanda."

"You're early today." Wanda hobbled to one side to let them in. "Did they fire you or did you quit?"

Corinne chuckled. "Neither. I...uh..."

She could not say it. Not in front of Dahlia. Not in front of anyone.

However, someone was bound to find out eventually. She could hide her tummy under a baggy shirt for only so long. Winter was coming when she could cover up with a coat or jacket, but winter was mild in these parts. It would look weird if she bulked up.

"You what?" Wanda didn't let up.

"I didn't feel well, so Sandra let me go. I will have to make up for the lost hours these two days one way or another."

Corinne could not say that she had seen a ghost from her past.

Oh, the irony.

She had ghosted Martin. And yet he had found her.

"Are you sick again? You've been sick these past several weeks."

"Might be something I ate."

"Or you're worn out." Wanda frowned. "I'm sorry. Maybe you can get a job with better pay so that you don't have to work as much. What happened to the restaurant job you had? You said the customers tipped a lot."

Corinne didn't want to be reminded of that darkness in this life. Why was it that every time something good happened to her, it had to be counteracted with something bad?

Strangely enough, she was not worried that Flavian had found her. Maybe she was two years removed from her past with Flavian, so she was able to look at the situation objectively. While Flavian was a violent man towards his enemies, at least he provided her with food and shelter. And he loved Dahlia.

Only he didn't love Dahlia's mother.

Used her, he did, for his own personal gains. Flavian's treatment of Corinne might be why his business partner had no respect for her either.

It was just as well that we left Flavian.

She corrected herself. *She* left Flavian. Dahlia had no say in it.

Wanda was muttering something that Corinne didn't hear. She didn't bother to ask Wanda to repeat. Let her mumble.

Frail and elderly, Wanda needed a tenant after her husband passed away. Corinne found two jobs in the thick of summer tourist season to help her pay for the room rental.

Wanda also threw in some perks, such as free childcare for Dahlia. In return, Corinne cleaned her house and provided company for the lonely widow.

Wanda also took Corinne and Dahlia to church. The preschool friends that Dahlia made in Sunday school were precious.

And then Corinne got saved. Once again, it was Wanda who had led her to the Lord.

How could she leave Wanda when she had been so kind to her?

Corinne locked the front and back doors. The wood looked flimsy. Anyone could break down these doors. Yet, Corinne still double-checked it, praying that God would protect them.

She glanced out the front windows. No cars there.

She wondered what Slam and Slime meant by keeping watch over her house. Where would they hide their car where she could not see them?

She sighed and prayed for God to keep her family safe.

When she turned around to check on Dahlia, she saw Wanda winced as she walked toward the small kitchen, where dishes had piled in the sink.

They didn't have a dishwasher any more, but Corinne preferred to hand-wash the dishes while she pondered life and prayed about her string of bad misfortunes.

Wanda made hissing sounds as she leaned on her wobbly cane.

"Your hips okay?" Corinne asked.

Several months ago, Wanda was complaining that her hips hurt.

"It's my knees this time. I might need to replace them."

"Is that what the doctor said—knee surgery?" Corinne made a beeline for the kitchen sink. She put on one of Wanda's old aprons, and began to sort the dishes.

"I want to put it off as long as possible."

"And suffer the whole way there?" Corinne filled a basin with soap and water.

Wanda laughed.

No, I cannot leave her. Corinne's eyes stung. She knew that if she and Dahlia left Key Largo, they'd have to take Wanda with them.

A life on the run wouldn't suit the eighty-nine-year-old.

Still, Flavian had found her. If he did, then Nikos wasn't too far behind.

Corinne knew she needed a champion.

Well, anyone but Martin.

Corinne didn't know how she got herself into such a mess. As she scrubbed the pots and pans in the sink, she prayed. At first, she rambled. Then her prayer became more desperate.

Please, God of heaven, I beg You to get me out of this mess.

Tears dripped into the sink, mixing in with the dishwater.

Forgive me, Lord. Help me. Protect my daughter. She's innocent. She did nothing wrong. Don't let my past mistakes harm her.

She prayed the same prayer on repeat the rest of the afternoon and into the evening, when she made them sandwiches for dinner and washed the plates again.

After watching some cartoons with Dahlia,

Corinne heated up some canned soup for the three of them. They shared some crackers. Then each had a banana and slices of peaches.

After Dahlia changed into her thrift-shop pajamas, Wanda read the Bible to both of them in the living room. The ceiling light was dim because one of the two lightbulbs had gone out.

There was no money to replace the bulbs until Corinne got paid. Then she could pay Wanda the rent. And Wanda could buy a lightbulb.

When they all said "Amen!" together, Corinne thanked God again in her heart for bringing Wanda into their lives.

God had sent Wanda for such a time as this.

If not for Wanda, both Corinne and her daughter would still be unchurched. No Bible studies for kids. No salvation in Christ.

Of course, it wasn't the church that had saved Corinne. However, it was in church that she had heard the Gospel message of how Jesus paid for all her sins—past, present, and future.

Jesus Christ was her rescuer.

Corinne wondered what her future would look like now that she was a believer.

And what could have happened if she hadn't left Savannah four years ago. Would she still have gotten saved at some point?

She had been saving up her salary from Tina's Turn to go to a four-year college. Maybe get an accounting degree or something substantial. She had a certificate from a community college, but had always wanted to go to university. Maybe even go to graduate school.

All those hopes and dreams shattered when Martin had something else in mind. His newfound faith caused him to make the rash decision of forcing her to move out of their apartment and then offering her marriage to absolve his guilt.

I wasn't ready for any of that.

They had sinned together, but Martin had cast her away.

Ironically, four years later, Corinne herself was also a Christian now. She had asked God to forgive her for sleeping with Martin—albeit before either one of them became believers of Jesus Christ.

According to the pastor at Wanda's church, when she sincerely asked God to forgive her, He would.

Psalm 103:12 drove the point home for Corinne.

As she carried the sleepy Dahlia down the hallway to their small bedroom, Corinne remembered the verse, and whispered it in her daughter's ear. "Sweet one, remember this: 'As far as the east is from the west, so far has He removed our transgressions from us.' When you grow up, maybe you will understand the forgiving love of God more fully."

So. Is there hope left for Martin and me?

Why else would he come to town?

CHAPTER SIX

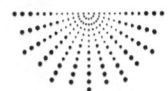

It was too hot outside. Instead of walking off the fudge he ate, Martin took a nap, waking up long after the sun had set and the moon had risen over the ocean—to a text message from his sister Tina.

Martin washed his face and called her back. She was resting in her sunroom, she said, with her two-year-old, while Byron Moss was down the hall in his home office, preparing for his Bible Study lessons at church.

Martin was happy for his sister's joyous marriage four years ago—one day after he became a Christian and one day before Corinne walked out on him.

"How did it go?" Tina asked. "I waited all afternoon for you to call."

"I took a nap and just got up."

"How long is the nap?"

"I don't know." Martin checked his phone. "Wow. It's nine o'clock. I can't believe I slept so much. Six hours."

"You must be tired from all that driving."

"Yeah. Must be. Now I could be up all night." He yawned. "Or not."

Martin could hear his niece laughing in the background. He padded to the couch by the sliding glass door that led to a small balcony facing the ocean.

Slowly, he explained what had transpired at the Key Largo Chocolate Shop, how Corinne took one look at him entering the shop and passed out in front of everybody.

"Don't give yourself too much credit," Tina said.

"Okay, let me add that she had been sitting outside in the hot sun eating lunch just before I entered the store. Maybe the sun was too hot and made her pass out. I think she needs to see a doctor to sort it out."

"That's not your job, is it?" Tina asked. "It's her problem if she needs to see a doctor."

Martin wondered if he should make it his problem.

Tina didn't give him time to think. She had already moved on to the next question. "What are you going to do?"

"I'll go back to the shop tomorrow." Martin wondered about the futility of such an action.

"What if she doesn't want to see you?"

"That happened today."

"Will tomorrow make any difference?"

"Maybe I scared her." Martin sighed. "I don't want to cause her trouble. I just want to talk."

"The Corinne I knew was pretty tough—except for that time when she passed out in your hospital room."

"You told me."

"I'm glad you're not riding motorcycles anymore, little brother. I hated to see her in such a state when we had no idea if you were going to live or die after that stupid wreck."

Martin shifted on the couch. "I'm into muscle cars now. Besides, I can carry more people in a car."

"Like an ex-girlfriend?"

"Truth be told, I don't know what I want anymore, Tina."

"You want a happy family. You told me that."

"What is happiness? What is joy?"

"You know, those are two different things."

"According to your dear husband."

"Right. He preached on that a few Sunday nights ago," Tina said. "You can still stream the sermon online from the church audio archives."

"I might do that." Martin drew a deep breath. "I felt nervous when I saw Corinne. I was neither happy nor sad. I didn't know what to think."

"Are you calming down now?"

"I don't think so. I left the store with over a pound of assorted fudge."

Tina laughed over the phone.

"It's only funny to you," Martin said.

"I'm sorry. I'm sure the store felt better about you being a customer than someone whom Corinne didn't want to see."

Martin got up from the couch and went to the sliding glass door. He opened it. Immediately a whiff of hot air blew into his face. He closed the door and returned to his couch.

He turned on the speakerphone and stretched out on the couch. "How is it going over there?"

"Same thing every day. Church, family, work."

Twice this week, Martin had already asked about her pottery studio in Atlanta. He wasn't going to ask about it again unless Tina wanted to volunteer new information.

She didn't.

"I better let you go in case your little one wants to take a nap," Martin said.

"She already did. It was a very short nap, no more than an hour."

"So I'm not taking up your time?"

"No, not at all. However, I suggest we pray about the situation and ask for God's help," Tina said. "I don't know what to tell you. I don't know whether you should go back to the shop tomorrow or send her a letter or what. However, God knows how to handle this. Pray and He will guide you."

"I've already prayed and I will pray again, but will you pray for me?"

"Most certainly. How about now?"

"Now is good." Martin loved hearing his sister's prayers because she prayed with confidence and she always sprinkled her prayers with praises to God and thanksgiving for what He had done in their lives. Martin knew he needed to learn to pray like that.

Before he knew it, Tina had said *amen*.

"Call Dad when you have a minute, will you?" Tina asked.

"Is he back from his auto show?" Martin hadn't called Dad since he left for Myrtle Beach to show off his latest muscle car acquisitions to curious onlookers.

"He's on his way back. According to his texts, he was thrilled for the new clients he had snapped up. They all wanted souped-up this or that."

That meant Dad needed Martin back in town to handle some of those accounts. Martin was glad that his days of working as a virtual assistant had worked out. "I'll call him. See if he needs me to work remotely."

"That can only mean one thing—you're not sure when you'll be back in town."

"Busted." Martin thought he might stay an extra week if he could talk to Corinne. "If Corinne won't talk to me, I'll be home sooner."

"I don't mean to add to your issues, but Dad has been hinting that he wants to retire."

"He said that?" Martin sat up. "I'm not ready for him to retire."

"He didn't say it himself but I get the sense that he's tired and wants to take it easy."

"Oh."

"I don't want MacMuscles and I'm not moving back to Savannah any time soon," Tina said. "Byron and I are raising our child here in metro Atlanta."

MacMuscles Classic Car Restoration belonged to Martin and his father, not to Tina, so

Martin did not expect Dad to just hand it over to anyone—even if Tina was a businesswoman herself.

"Pray about it so that you will be ready with an answer if he asks you," Tina added.

"If?"

"You know how Dad is. He may not want to give it up just yet."

"He doesn't have to give up anything." Martin thought that Dad was more of a control freak than Mom—who had passed away many years ago.

"Even if he retires, he wants to call the shots," Tina reminded him.

"That, he does. Damaris will keep him in check though." Their stepmother had a good head on her shoulders.

"However, we know that when he needs help, he wants it at the drop of a hat," Tina added. "So don't stay away too long. I'm not going to Savannah to cover for you."

"I know." Martin knew he had to tell Dad soon about his supposedly two-week road trip.

Martin wished he had told Dad right away that he was only driving as far as Key Largo. As far as Dad was concerned, Martin could have been multiple states away from Georgia, not only next door.

"Why is it that I have a feeling you didn't tell him everything?" Tina asked.

"Well, I didn't know myself what was going to happen when I arrived." It was the truth.

His first encounter with Corinne had ended abruptly when she passed out right before his eyes without as much as a hello.

Would there be another encounter?

What if Corinne disappeared again?

CHAPTER SEVEN

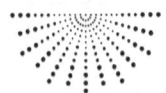

"o, I didn't get a chance. She was whisked away." Martin turned up his phone volume so he could hear what Ming would say next. He placed the phone on his armrest. The dashboard was warming up, even with the air-conditioner blasting inside the car.

As he waited, he sipped iced coffee in a giant paper cup. Key Largo was warming up all around the car on this Friday morning, to the point that Martin wondered if the paper cup would hold up with all that condensation. The coffee shop he had gone to didn't have plastic cups, and their giant-sized mugs were too expensive.

Martin might be the Vice President of MacMuscles, but it didn't mean he was going to spend twenty dollars on a collector's mug. Collector cars, maybe.

The road in front of Key Largo Chocolate Shop was busy today, with weekenders pouring into town for a break. Martin's eyes were on the front door, but Corinne hadn't come out at all.

"I'm not sure if it's a good idea for you to sit there waiting for her to show up." Ming's voice came through fairly clearly on the phone.

Martin was going to use video, but his signal was weak in this part of town. He made a mental note to change carrier. If he drove another mile, his phone switched to roaming. Every little cost added up.

"Employees usually don't use the same entrances as customers," Ming added.

"I know. But it's almost eleven o'clock, and maybe she'll come outside for lunch again." It was Martin's excuse, and he wanted to stick by the story.

"If someone complains or says anything about stalking, it's a lot of trouble for you."

"I'm not stalking."

Ming didn't reply.

"Say something." Martin shifted in his seat.

"I told you earlier, when you first called me and said you're already in Key Largo." Ming's voice was emotionless. "I wish you had waited for me to get more information. Like I said, I'm waiting on someone to get back to me. Remember how I said I'd have something for you on Tuesday next week?"

Might as well confess. "I didn't have the nerve to tell you where I am."

"You felt guilty that you jumped the gun."

"Now Corinne knows I'm in town." Martin wasn't sure how that might have changed the dynamics of their entire situation.

"Patience is a fruit of the Holy Spirit," Ming reminded him.

"Well, to be fair to myself, Thursday was just this side of the weekend heading toward Tuesday." Martin wasn't sure whether his friend would buy that. "Today is Friday. Even closer to Tuesday."

"No, Martin. Thursday was five days away from Tuesday. Today is four days from Tuesday. You just end up paying for extra hotel when you could have waited."

"What were you planning to do?" Martin asked. He had asked Ming that before, but the latter wouldn't say.

"I had to brainstorm some ideas with my associates in Florida. I didn't want to tell you prematurely if it doesn't work out."

"If what doesn't work out?"

"Stay away from Corinne for now. Why don't you go back to your hotel room while I dig around a bit more about her situation?"

Now Ming was saying it again: wait.

"Okay."

Martin wondered how frail Corinne's health was if she fainted at the first sight of him.

She didn't look frail or skinny—the baggy clothes hid everything—and she didn't look sickly either.

This morning, Martin went to the shop as soon as it opened at nine o'clock. He tried to find out when Corinne—Dinah—worked, but nobody would tell him. All they said was that she doesn't work on Sundays, and even that was too much information.

That made Martin wonder. Why wouldn't Corinne work on Sundays? She wasn't a Christian, was she? In fact, some Christians worked on Sundays too.

Ming said he had to go. "Don't do anything else I wouldn't do."

Martin didn't want to second-guess his friend, but what could Ming find out for him all the way from Savannah when he, Martin, was already here. Boots on the ground.

Martin had an idea of what he wanted to do.

He wasn't sure if it was something God would want him to do—or that God would approve—but it seemed to be a waste of his time if he went back to the hotel room and waited for hours for Ming to call again.

Technically, Ming was right.

Martin should have stayed in Savannah until Ming had more information.

Now that Corinne had seen him, she might run again.

And then Martin would be back to where he started: without her.

He said goodbye to Ming and hung up his phone. He drank the rest of the now-diluted iced coffee, glanced at the analog clock on the dashboard, and prayed for wisdom.

CHAPTER EIGHT

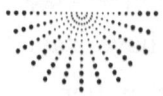

*A*nother hour passed by, and Martin was still sitting in his car. He listened to the twelve o'clock local news, but turned it off at the first commercial.

His stomach rumbled, and he had to go to the bathroom.

Martin could not imagine what it would be like to run surveillance for real—what Ming and the Savannah River Investigations firm did all the time. Now, Helen Hu's private investigation firm was more international, but Martin guessed the work was mostly mundane.

Sit in the vehicle and watch someone show up.

That's not me.

He picked up his empty coffee cup and his

phone, and climbed out of the car. He locked the doors, double-checking to make sure he really did, and then crossed the busy street.

The girl he had talked to earlier this morning wasn't there. Just as well. Martin didn't want to cause her any trouble with her manager.

He saw a familiar-looking guy at the checkout. He was the same person who had taken Corinne home the day before—or at least, given her a ride somewhere.

Martin wondered if he should talk to him.

Then he spotted the fifty-something woman who had helped Corinne the moment she hit the floor on Thursday afternoon. She seemed to be in charge.

Martin looked around the store, hoping to see a notice board. He swiped his phone and googled the store to see if there were any job openings.

None.

The crowd thinned out a bit. Martin stepped over to where the lady was.

"Excuse me," he said.

"May I help you?" Upon closer look, she had lines on her face, but her eyes were bright and shiny. Her hair was salt-and-pepper and wiry.

"Yes, I'm hoping you can help me. I was here

yesterday, but due to the commotion, I wasn't able to talk to you."

"I remember you. You're a friend of Dinah's?"

"Long ago, when we were young." Not too young, but nobody asked for the exact time and date. "Anyway, I'm going to be in town for the rest of summer, and I was wondering if you have job openings."

"All our positions are filled, but if you send in your resume, I'll call you if anything opens up," she said. "I'm Sandra Preston."

"Owner?" Martina asked.

"Yes. What type of work are you looking for?"

"Anything part-time, if possible. I worked for years as a virtual assistant." Martin was being truthful here. He had worked as a virtual assistant all the way through college and then some. After that, he became his sister's personal assistant in her busy tri-city pottery studio.

After his last motorcycle accident, his dad showed up in town and hired him to do office work for him while he tried to build up his muscle car restoration business. Three years later, Dad promoted him to vice president and gave him a minority ownership of the business.

Martin knew that he wasn't going to get an

entry-level or minimum-wage job by touting his VP position.

"Virtual assistant? Like an office manager?" Sandra asked.

"It can be. Mostly I do scheduling, inventory, time management, social media updates, news briefs, blog posts. I can also do other office work, if needed."

"Interesting. Wait here and I'll get you a job application form," she said.

"Okay. Thank you." Martin prayed that he hadn't made a mistake. He didn't want to turn away —or turn off—Corinne.

Sandra came back quickly. The application form was wrinkled at one edge. "Fill that out and attach your resume."

"I'll get it back to you after lunch."

"That soon?"

"Yeah. I'm here, and I could start work today. I'll just need to find a place to print my resume."

Sandra gave him a look.

Martin tried not to look desperate.

"Well, I'm too busy today, and it's already Friday. We're very busy on weekends. I won't be able to get to your application until Monday," Sandra said.

Next week?

Martin prayed quietly for God to give him patience to wait three days. "That's fine."

"You know, you might be able to use the printer at the library." Sandra told him where it was located. "They're usually open until six o'clock, except for a day or two. They're closed on Sundays, so you have today and tomorrow to fill out your forms."

"Good to know. Thanks for the information." Martin smiled. "So when I'm done with it, how do I drop off my paperwork?"

"I'm here the rest of the day." She seemed doubtful that Martin would return today. "I'm working for only half a day tomorrow, so if you get here before noon, you can drop it off with me. Otherwise it'll have to be Monday. Or you can drop it off at the mailbox outside."

Martin had no idea where the mailbox was. Sandra pointed in the general direction of the front door, which was open wide now with customers pouring in.

"When do you leave town?" Sandra asked.

"In a couple of months."

"So you can only work here for two months?"

"Actually, as a virtual assistant, I could work remotely from anywhere. I'm not geography-dependent."

"I see. Where are you from originally?"

"Savannah, Georgia."

"Just passing through?" Her eyebrows rose.

"I'm taking a solo road trip, driving my dad's car on the open road. I could keep going all the way until Key Largo if I want."

"And telecommute?"

"Yep." Although Martin was beginning to doubt if he could technically go back to his old virtual assistant job now that he was VP at MacMuscles.

That could be a problem if Dad wanted him home any time sooner. He figured he could talk Dad into letting him do work remotely. If he had to drive home to Savannah for the weekend, he could. It would be a little over five hundred and fifty miles. Or about eight hours of driving non-stop. He could do it.

All because he wanted to talk to Corinne again.

What on earth am I doing?

At the back of Martin's mind, he wondered if asking for her forgiveness was the only thing he had come all the way to Key Largo for.

What if I want more?

CHAPTER NINE

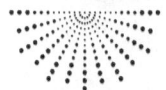

*C*orinne got up before dawn on Saturday morning to read her Bible and pray. By the time she made coffee and carried her Bible to the back porch, the sun was rising.

She sat on the rickety chair that probably needed to be cleaned with bleach soon. The porch also needed sweeping.

Maybe she could do that before she went to work today.

The thought of work reminded her of who had walked into the Key Largo Chocolate Shop on Thursday afternoon.

Why did God allow Martin to find her in Key Largo?

That had to be the only reason he was in town.

Four years, and he still hadn't forgotten her.

Oddly enough, she felt a sense of relief that he had found her. Two years ago, she wouldn't have thought she'd survive to raise her daughter.

If something should happen to her...

She held back her tears.

Tropical birds chirped in the neighborhood trees. Corinne looked up to see leaves rustling in the morning wind.

Sparrows landed on a chain-link fence near a two-piece birdbath that Corinne had salvaged from someone's trash and hauled five blocks home, one piece at a time. Dahlia enjoyed filling that birdbath with tap water, but it had been during one of her chore times that she stepped on an anthill.

All was well now, and Corinne had taken care of that anthill and all the ants in it. She felt sorry for the ants she had to kill, but sorrier for her daughter who was allergic to ants, it turned out.

The sparrows drank from the birdbath.

They reminded Corinne of verses from the New Testament. She looked them up in her Bible that someone at church had given to her when she was saved. She found the verses in Luke 12:6-7.

Are not five sparrows sold for two farthings, and not one of them is forgotten before God? But even the very hairs of your head are all numbered. Fear not therefore: ye are of more value than many sparrows.

A stream of tears streaked down her red cheeks.

"I am more valuable than many sparrows. Thank You, Jesus."

Corinne knew that trouble hadn't left her, not even after she became a Christian. Trouble was only a door knock away.

Would God send help?

She lifted her eyes to the sky as another verse came to her mind. This time it was from Psalm 102:7, a verse Wanda had mentioned to her before.

I lie awake,

   And am like a sparrow alone on the housetop.

The back door creaked open. "Mommy?"

Corinne quickly wiped her eyes on the back of her hand. She drew a deep breath.

"Yes, baby?" She smiled broadly.

It wasn't that she didn't want her daughter to see her cry, but it was too much to explain. And too soon for the little girl to comprehend life's complex problems.

"Are you going to work today at the chocolate shop?" Dahlia asked.

"Yes." Corinne motioned for Dahlia to sit on her lap.

"Can you get me some chocolate? And for Aunt Wanda too?"

"I will. You take good care of Aunt Wanda when I'm at work today, okay?"

Dahlia nodded.

Corinne brushed a fine strand of hair from Dahlia's face. Her straight but wispy hair was getting long. Next week, Corinne would give her a haircut. It saved money that way.

Dahlia leaned into Corinne and gave her a hug. "I love you very much, Mommy."

"I love you too, baby."

Since she had given birth to Dahlia, Corinne knew that she would do everything she could to protect her child.

Everything.

Lord, help me.

Was it time for them to disappear again?

CHAPTER TEN

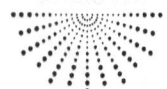

*W*alking among the coconut trees and getting sand in his flip-flops, Martin waited for a phone call or email from Sandra Preston at the chocolate shop. He had been up since seven o'clock, watching the sunrise from beach, and then driving to breakfast at an old restaurant Dad had told him about.

Behind the restaurant, the sand stretched all the way to the Atlantic Ocean, interrupted here and there by coconut trees, hammocks, and tourists taking pictures. At the beach, Martin took in the panorama, thanking God for a beautiful day.

The scene reminded him of his sister Tina's wedding on Moss Cay in the Bahamas. Corinne had accompanied him. It was tense between them because Martin got his own hotel room, and Corinne mistook him for wanting to play the field.

It all came to a head two days later when Martin finally explained to Corinne about his conversion to Christianity. Corinne didn't understand what the big deal was. People of different faiths had built families together, hadn't they? Why couldn't Martin just put aside his religiosity and make her happy?

Needless to say, they broke up. It was inevitable. Martin suddenly found himself at odds with Corinne. He wanted to know more about God, read the Bible more deeply, and attend church more regularly.

Everywhere he turned, he found himself looking at the stark difference between Christianity and secularism, between life in Christ and life in the world.

There was no way he could reconcile.

Perhaps, in addition to asking Corinne to forgive him, Martin could give her a tract or a Bible.

He wished he had brought more than his own personal study Bible, but if he had to, he would give that to her. It had verses underlined, which could be useful to her.

If she wanted it.

On the other hand, Martin could also find a

Christian store—or even WalMart—and buy her a Bible.

Yeah, I'll do that.

It was a safer route.

That way, he didn't have to give up his Bible—in case all Corinne was going to do was throw it in the trash can.

Still, Martin wondered what she was doing now.

The sun rose up. Martin donned his sunglasses, feeling pleased with himself that he didn't need to go to work today. He could just enjoy his vacation.

Unfortunately, he had done something rash—apply for a job at the same chocolate shop that Corinne worked in.

All for the purpose of getting close enough to her to ask her to forgive him for sinning against her and God four years ago.

And to find out if Corinne was still searching for an answer to her life's problems.

Search no more, Corinne. God is near.

*A*fter his lone beach walk, Martin walked back to his hotel room behind the coconut grove to find a woman waiting for him outside his door.

"Martin MacFarland?" She handed him a plastic business card that looked more like a credit card.

Martin studied it, wondering if it could be a marketing idea for MacMuscles. They could have theirs cut out in the shape of a muscle car, for example.

Finally, he read the words.

Private Investigator Pilar Santiago.

"You're the associate in Miami." Martin stretched out his hand.

Pilar didn't shake his hand. "Ming Wei sent me."

"Yeah?" Martin didn't believe her. After all, Ming had said he wouldn't get back to him until Tuesday. "Call Ming right now on your phone and let me talk to him."

So she did, and put Ming on speakerphone. "Mr. MacFarland here wants to verify that you sent me."

"Hey, Martin!" It was Ming. "Why are you interrupting my Saturday morning coffee?"

"She said you sent her. But it's not Tuesday."

Holding the phone, Pilar chuckled.

"I texted you, dude," Ming said.

Martin checked his own phone. Sure enough, there was a long text from Ming saying that Pilar was going to take it from here. "I see. I was out walking. Didn't hear a thing."

"Too much ocean?" Ming asked, but didn't wait for Martin to respond. "I have an emergency job I have to do this afternoon. I will be gone for at least a month."

"Something more important than my situation?" Martin asked, almost sarcastically.

"In a word, yes. I can't go into details, but you'll be happy to know I'm picking up Pilar's tab."

"Good." Martin still didn't like it.

"Emergency rate," Ming said, as if driving in the point.

"How much?" Might as well ask.

Ming told him.

Martin's eyes widened. "By the hour?"

Pilar nodded. "I've been here for an hour, waiting for you to finish your morning walk on the beach. Add fifteen minutes of your questioning who I am... Let's just say the clock is ticking fast."

"Wow. Thanks, Ming." Martin sat down.

"I'm sorry for the sudden change of plans, but

Pilar's got it."

"What's the plan, Ming?" Martin asked.

"Tell me you're not outdoors somewhere, calling me in an open space with WiFi everywhere."

Martin reached for his hotel room key. "We can talk inside."

After Pilar stepped into his hotel room, Martin locked it.

"Ming, you still there?" Pilar was still holding her cell phone.

"Yeah." Ming's voice came through just fine on the speakerphone.

"Want some water? That's all I have." Martin walked to the small refrigerator in the cabinet under the television.

"No, thanks. I've got water in my car." Pilar sat down in the lone armchair without being invited.

"What's the plan?" Martin sat on the queen bed. Somewhere at the back of his mind, he wondered what Corinne would say if she found him here with a woman who was not his sister or stepmother.

Then again, this was business. And Ming was on the phone.

"Stay away from the Key Largo Chocolate

Shop." Pilar's voice hardened. "Let me get to know Dinah for a few days. See what's going on."

"And how are you planning on doing that?" Martin asked.

"Already got the ball rolling," Ming replied.

"I thought you said to wait until Tuesday."

"Well, after we talked on the phone, I was afraid you'd go do something incredibly ill-advised," Ming said. "You know, like applying for a job at the chocolate shop."

Martin nearly choked on his water. "How did you know?"

"No comment," Ming and Pilar said in unison.

Martin raised an eyebrow. He could have raised both eyebrows, but that would give away the fact that he was surprised that Ming was doing his job. Along with that, Martin would have to admit his lack of knowledge regarding matters related to private investigations.

"I start work tomorrow," Pilar continued.

"Tomorrow? Corinne doesn't work on Sundays," Martin said.

"Exactly why I start tomorrow. They need someone to fill in for her—this being a busy summer, you know. I'm happy to work at minimum wage."

Martin frowned. He pursed his lips. He

wanted to be the one working there with Corinne.

Then again, his presence at the store could scare her off and she'd run again.

"The chocolate shop opens at noon on Sundays," Pilar said. "I'll leave the church service fifteen minutes early. I don't expect to stay here for more than two weeks. After that, I'll be gone."

Martin wanted to say that he didn't care what she did with her own free time, but he didn't want to get on the wrong side of a PI who was helping him to reconnect with Corinne.

"If you're looking for a church to attend, there's one about fifteen minutes from here. Google Beach Town Church. Pastor Butler." Pilar smiled—almost slyly. "It's a tiny church—and frankly, the building on the website looks like it needs a new paint job—but one Dinah Miller is singing in an ensemble tomorrow morning at eleven."

Corinne?

Somewhat shocked, Martin tried to remain calm.

"Nonetheless, we can't be seen together, so from now on, separate cars. Text me or Ming or call if you need anything."

Martin barely nodded.

Corinne singing in church?

It was all he could think of the rest of the day.

CHAPTER ELEVEN

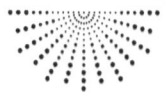

*W*anda's church was so small that
sometimes they met behind the
Christian-owned gift and tackle shop next door that
closed on Sundays. The parking lot was empty all
the way to the shady trees, but it was too hot for the
congregation to meet under the bright morning sun,
so they took their camp and folding chairs to the
grassy patch that separated the parking lot from the
beach.

Corinne looked up when she heard a truck
door slam. She watched the woman get out of the
bright red Chevy.

"Pilar!" Corinne waved, pointing to an empty
spot near her. Corinne wanted to be friendly with
new hires at work. She didn't know for sure where

Pilar stood spiritually, but she had accepted Corinne's invitation to church, and that was a good start.

Today there were maybe fifty people in attendance at the church service. The nursery workers had taken the kids down to the beach for their children's church.

Corinne would rather Dahlia stay with her throughout the church service, but this was how Wanda's church worked. Some day, when Corinne found a place to settle down, she would find a church where families worshipped together.

Wanda went to sit with her friends in the front row so they could hear the preacher better. They weren't the only ones who missed Pastor Butler when he took his family to the Grand Canyon on a summer vacation to celebrate the high school graduation of his firstborn son.

Corinne also missed his preaching, but it looked like he was going to pick up where he had left off two weeks ago.

His wife, Chiyoko, came over to see Corinne just as Pilar reached her as well. Corinne introduced them to each other.

"I'm on diet, but I always make an exception for chocolate," Chiyoko said.

As Pilar chatted with the pastor's wife, Corinne

heard another vehicle door shut. She turned, and froze.

What is he doing here?

How does he know I attend this church?

Her mind went blank.

Truly, she should have expected Martin to hang around. He had arrived on Thursday and visited the chocolate shop. She had called in sick on Friday.

On Saturday, Sandra had called Corinne into her office to ask about Martin's application for job at the chocolate shop. Corinne had come clean— mostly—with Sandra, telling her that Martin was an ex-boyfriend who was probably just passing through town.

And yes, even though he was harmless, Corinne explained that she would feel uncomfortable if Sandra hired him to work in the office.

Sandra then rejected Martin's application and tossed it in the trash can.

Now he is here. In my church.

Who told him about this church?

Could it be Pilar? She had arrived in Key Largo two days after Martin did.

Corinne glanced over at Pilar.

Who is she, really?

The only thing Corinne knew about Pilar was

that she was a fast learner, and would be filling in this afternoon for her and another worker who didn't work on Sundays.

Someone played a hymn on guitar, and Chiyoko said she had to go. Pilar sat down on the grass. She hadn't brought a chair.

Someone tapped Corinne on her shoulder. She turned to find Old Man Pete offering up his seat on the bench to Pilar.

"Thank you. That's very kind of you." Pilar sat down behind Corinne.

Old Man Pete walked to the back of the gathering, and stood by the trees where several other men were standing, sipping coffee and eating doughnuts that someone had brought.

Corinne looked over the lyrics she had folded and stashed into her Bible. She and the other four women only had to sing once, but it was one of her favorite hymns.

Of all days, Martin would hear her sing it.

Would he have many questions?

She couldn't offer him any answer—not the ones he probably sought.

She had willfully left Savannah four years ago. Left her old life behind. Gone into the seedy side of Las Vegas. Met a gambler who took a chance on her. Broke up with the man of violence to protect her daughter. Wandered around the country.

And ended up here.

Corinne knew she couldn't hide forever.

But there was no way she was going back to Martin. Her life had become too complicated. There was too much to unravel.

Martin wouldn't want her now.

She'd have to find a way to tell him that he had to let her go. She had moved on, but it seemed that he hadn't.

CHAPTER TWELVE

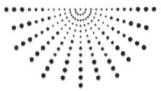

*L*eaning against a tree and listening to the congregation sing, their voices lifted into the open air, was something unexpected for Martin.

So this is what an outdoor church looks like.

"We usually meet next door," the man who called himself Pete said when everyone sat down after they finished singing. He pointed with his arthritic fingers.

Martin couldn't see anything beyond the trees.

The man who called himself Pete—

Actually, he said that his name was Old Man Pete.

Martin almost asked him how old he was,

because he didn't look too much older than Dad, who was in his seventies now.

Martin stared at the wrinkles on his face, tanned from the sun. His arms seemed dry.

"I know you're wanting to know how old I am," Pete said. "After about three heart attacks, I'm finally living my age. I'll be seventy five next month."

"But that's not why they call you Old Man Pete."

"No, I got that because I dispense free wisdom to anyone who cares to ask."

"Ah."

"I know much of what I usually say is common sense, but this church knows that a widower needs to feel useful."

"It's a ministry then," Martin said.

"Exactly."

The pastor made some announcements. A baby shower here, a hospice visit there.

Then Martin watched as five ladies went to the front. Corinne stood to one side. She never looked his way.

He dared not look at her either. He began to doubt himself, doubt his decision to come to Key Largo to get a glimpse of the woman he had lost.

She must be strong if she could stand there and sing while he was in the same space as she was.

Then again, her focus had to be on God and not on him.

> *This is my Father's world.*
> *O let me ne'er forget*
> *that though the wrong*
> *seems oft so strong,*
> *God is the ruler yet.*

Martin closed his eyes, listening along with the five-in-one ensemble. They didn't let Corinne sing solo but Martin could pick out her occasional soprano.

She used to sing in his shower—back in his unsaved days. And here she was, singing in church.

God can change anyone.

The hymn stuck in Martin's head all the way through the sermon, the benediction, and the dispersal of the church.

Don't let me forget, God, that You are still in charge.

"Well, it's good to meet you, Martin." Pete extended his hand.

Martin took one look at his hand and knew. "You work on cars?"

"Can you tell?" Pete wiped his hand on his cargo shorts. "I thought I got all that oil off."

"They're under your nails, in between the rough cracks in your hand."

Pete looked at both his hands, palm and back. "My wife—she's in heaven now—used to tell me to wear gloves."

"What kind of cars do you work on?" Martin asked.

"Old cars. Old trucks. I've been spending a lot of time on a 1959 Volkswagen bus."

"Wow. Did you restore it?"

"It's unfinished. My shop is in my backyard, and it's going to take a while. I have to scrounge around for tools."

He sounded like how Dad started out restoring classic cars. Car parts all over his car porch.

"What are you going to do with the bus when you get it restored?" Martin asked.

"I don't know. But my cardiologist said I needed to pick up a hobby that's not stressful."

"Restoring old vehicles is fun."

"Indeed. Other than the bus, I try to work on my Chevelle."

"A Chevy. What year?" Martin asked as they navigated through the small crowd of people standing around, just chatting.

Martin wanted to go get lunch before his stomach rumbled.

"Some of it was built in 1967, the rest 1969. I've been looking for parts. It's not cheap, this Malibu." Pete's eyes brightened. "You know anything about old cars?"

"A little bit." Not as much as Dad.

"When my friend died, his wife said I could have it if I could restore it the way her husband would have." Pete laughed. "The catch was she didn't send along some money to get it done."

"You got the car though."

"I got the car," Pete said. "And my friend's memories. We used to go deep-sea fishing together until his heart gave out and he didn't want to be too far away from land."

Martin let him talk as they walked to the parking lot. He didn't know what to say about that. Dad was getting up there in age too.

"Better enjoy life while we still can." It was all Martin could say.

He heard squeals and peals of laughter from a bunch of kids behind him. The nursery must have let out. He wondered where they put the kids, but didn't feel like he had any business asking.

"Mommy! Mommy!" The little girl's voice sounded like bells.

"Dahlia! Dahlia!" a woman responded.

Martin froze. That voice.

Slowly he turned around.

Corinne's back was toward him. Her arms were stretched out.

A little girl dressed in pretty pink, her wispy hair all askew, ran into those arms. She was about half the height of Corinne.

Tall for a girl who seemed to be about three years old.

I'm tall...

"My baby," Corinne said. "Did you have a good time in Sunday school?"

"Yes, Mommy. We sang a lot of songs about Jesus!"

Hug, hug. Kiss, kiss.

Then Corinne held the little girl's hand. They turned around and—

She froze.

Her eyes turned sad.

Like she was about to burst into tears.

She mumbled something that Martin couldn't hear.

"Mr. Pete!" Dahlia broke away from Corinne and ran toward Old Man Pete, who was still standing next to Martin, right in the middle of the parking lot.

That one line played back in Martin's mind as he turned his attention to the little girl—Dahlia was her name—now chatting away with Pete.

She looked like a miniature Corinne.

How old are you, little one?

Martin couldn't get the question out. The words choked in his throat. "This is My Father's World" played back in his mind.

Corinne walked toward them, slowly, as if trying not to stir him.

As she passed by him, she didn't say a word to him.

Martin stared at the back of her head.

"We have to go, baby," she said to her daughter. "Lunch is waiting for us."

Martin almost asked if he could join them.

"Who's cooking today?" Pete asked.

"Miss Angelina and friends." Corinne kept her voice down, as though she didn't want Martin to know about their plans.

Well, I'm a stranger here.

"Hey, Martin." Pete slapped his shoulder. "Why don't you join us? You can be my plus one."

Corinne blinked. She didn't say a word.

"I wanna be your plus one!" Dahlia lifted her arms in the air.

Pete chuckled. "Okay, you can be my plus one, and Martin can be my plus two."

"Is Mommy plus three then?" Dahlia let Pete hoist her in the air.

Martin tried not to freak out.

Am I a father?

CHAPTER THIRTEEN

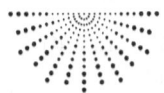

*T*he gathering at Angelina's boathouse near the marina was small, but the space suddenly felt stuffy, and Corinne wanted to leave. However, she couldn't because she had no car.

She, Dahlia, and Wanda would have to wait until they finished lunch and cleaned up the kitchen before Angelina could take them home.

There was no way she was going to get a ride from Old Man Pete, who had been asking questions about their origins—especially about Dahlia's unnamed father.

And not on this planet would she get a ride home from Martin—who shouldn't be here at all.

His presence caused her great discomfort.

If she thought Pete would ask questions, Martin would be even worse.

Corinne left Dahlia playing with Angelina's grandchildren in a small corner of the living room while she tried to make herself useful in the repainted galley kitchen.

The single sixty-something Angelina lived here alone, and had offered to rent one of her two bedrooms to Corinne about a year ago. Corinne had turned her down because she wanted Dahlia to have a real yard to play in, and she was afraid Dahlia would fall overboard into the dirty water of the canal.

"If you want to help, setting the table is all we have left to do," Angelina said.

Corinne nodded.

"Meat's been cooking in the crockpot since this morning, and the spaghetti's all boiled and done."

Corinne nodded again.

"Cat got your tongue?" Angelina laughed.

"I'm just tired, is all." Corinne didn't say more. She hadn't been throwing up in the morning in the last few days. Maybe she was entering the second trimester early—if there was such a thing.

"You need a nap too? I know I want one." Angelina pointed to a cabinet under the counter. "Will you hand me a colander from under there?"

"Sure." Corinne had been here before, so she knew where most of everything was in the kitchen.

After a few minutes of collecting mismatched forks and spoons, Corinne made her way to the living room, where a few people had set up the table.

From the corner of her eye, she saw Martin walking through the sliding glass door toward the patio and the dock.

Let him go.

She heard her heart say that, but her mind said she had better clear the air with him. Dahlia was not his and would never be his.

Corinne put the silverware down on the table and followed Martin out.

"Martin," she said quietly, hoping that he wouldn't hear her—then she didn't have to talk to him.

Unfortunately, Martin heard her. He stopped at the edge of the boat.

The sunlight bounced off his brown hair. His aviator sunglasses hid his eyes from her. He hesitated for a moment, and then took off his sunglasses.

"I'm sorry," he said.

How many times has he said that?

"I'm sorry too." Corinne stepped closer, but not too close.

"I know you don't want me in her life..."

"Whose life?"

"Your daughter."

"She's not yours." Corinne didn't want to start a fight, but she knew whose daughter Dahlia was. There was no doubt.

"You sure? A DNA test could..."

I wish you were her father. "Martin, I conceived her six months after I left Savannah."

Corinne could see the mixed emotions on his face. On the one hand, he looked relieved, but on the other hand, he looked perplexed.

"Where's the father then?" Martin's voice was harsh.

Corinne shook her head. "He must never know we're here."

"Why not?"

Corinne didn't know what to say. She prayed for wisdom. "Please."

"Something wrong?" Martin pressed.

"I go by Dinah Miller now..." Corinne wondered how much more to add to that.

Martin nodded slightly. "Whatever."

"A—are you staying for lunch?" Corinne asked.

Martin didn't answer.

"Angelina makes great spaghetti," Corinne added.

"I don't want to make you uncomfortable."

If there was one thing Corinne liked about Martin, it was his honesty. There was no way Flavian could measure up to Martin, ever.

"Please stay," Corinne said.

"You want me to?"

Corinne nodded.

But only for lunch.

~

Doing nothing but waiting alone in his hotel room wasn't Martin's idea of a beach vacation on Key Largo. There was nothing he wanted to do. Not boating, fishing, sunbathing, shopping, or anything else tourists did in the Florida Keys.

All he wanted was to have a long talk with Corinne about the last four years of their lives apart. Specifically, he wanted to know why Corinne was running from Dahlia's father—whoever he was.

And whether they had married.

In a way, Martin didn't want to know.

Not right now.

He also didn't want to know if he himself was truly Dahlia's biological father.

It's unthinkable, I know.

The lunch at Angelina's houseboat two hours ago had gone without a hitch. Martin had dutifully remembered to address Corinne as Dinah, or not at all.

Dahlia was a charming three-year-old who seemed to be a happy child, without a care in the world. She had faint red patches all over her arms and legs, which had something to do with ant bites, as Martin was told by several church members.

Martin didn't remember how he was like at that age. Had he gotten into trouble? Fallen onto an ant hill?

He didn't recall.

Dressed in a wrinkled tee-shirt he had grabbed from the dryer on Thursday and didn't take out of his suitcase until just now, Martin stretched out on the rattan lounger by the sliding glass door that overlooked the sandy grove of coconut trees.

The trees loomed above his small deck, and he thought he could reach up and touch the green coconuts.

But it was hot outside, and he'd rather sit here and do nothing.

He had brought his Bible from Savannah. He

had read it this morning during his personal quiet time with God. He had paid attention in that little church.

Without a doubt, God had brought him here for such a time as this.

Perhaps all he would be able to do was to make peace with Corinne and then move on with his life.

But he had to know.

Martin closed his eyes in the cool room, enjoying the air-conditioner at full blast.

He knew he had to call Dad. He told his sister he would.

He also probably should call Pastor Flores.

And Ming.

And Tina again.

Martin knew he needed all the help he could get.

Then again, Corinne might need more help than he did.

He had no idea where she lived, but she had no car, worked a minimum wage job, was a single mother with a daughter to feed, living under an assumed name, and did not want her ex-partner to know where she was.

Martin could pretty much guess that no one in Key Largo knew her real name.

How long could she go on like that?

CHAPTER FOURTEEN

*F*ifteen minutes before noon every day except Sunday, Corinne had to sit outside on the bench facing the traffic. Somewhere across the street, Flavian's men would watch her.

It was the strangest agreement, but it was the only thing that Flavian had offered her to keep her unborn child and her three-year-old safe.

Corinne put on her sunglasses and opened her lunch bag. Peanut butter and jelly sandwich again today. It was pretty much all she could afford. She knew she should be eating more for the baby, but a meal plan wasn't included in their deal.

Sometimes Corinne wondered if she should have just called Flavian and gotten it over with. Let

Flavian and Nikos duke it out. Let them settle their differences—while she ran.

Where to?

She touched the bracelet on her left hand. It was still there, plastic and wood beads strung together. It looked cheap—which was the whole idea—but her FBI handler said she had to keep it on her at all times. If she was separated from her bracelet, an alarm would go off somewhere, and her handler would come running to her rescue.

She closed her eyes.

I want to be safe all the time, without any need to be rescued at all.

Corinne said grace over her lunch and added, "And Lord, runners may say they're tired of running, but my journey is not over. Help me find someone who can take care of Dahlia and this little baby."

Someone who doesn't mind that my children came from different fathers, one consensual, one forced.

Both men should be in jail for their own reasons, if Corinne had anything to do with it.

The sun moved.

Or a shadow appeared.

A voice spoke.

"Corinne." That familiar voice that had once

been soothing to her in bed four years ago now sounded like metal grating metal.

Martin MacFarland.

Without looking at him, Corinne gritted her teeth as she replied. "You cannot be here."

"But I am." The voice came closer.

Corinne kept her eyes on the street.

"You put both of us in danger if you come here."

"Danger? How?"

Corinne took another bite of her sandwich. Chewed it slowly.

The shadow didn't go away.

Corinne swallowed. "Don't come any closer. They already see you."

"They who?" When Corinne didn't say, he continued. "I was at church yesterday. Did they see me then? And what about at Angelina's houseboat?"

"We have many visitors at church."

"Exactly. So I happen to be in town and here we are, meeting at the bench. How do you do?"

Corinne put her sandwich back into her lunch bag. "Ask me for directions."

"To your heart?"

Corinne nearly laughed. "To a place in town, silly."

Before Martin could reply, Corinne put down her lunch bag. Looked up at him.

He was wearing a faded tee-shirt with some sort of design on it, tucked into a pair of shorts. He didn't wear any sunglasses.

His eyes were pained.

"I thought we had a good time on Sunday," he said softly.

Corinne stood up, and walked toward him. She pointed far away down the street, waving her arms as though she was giving directions. "Walk two blocks over there, and then turn the corner."

"You're not wearing a wedding ring," Martin whispered. "I noticed that yesterday."

"I'm pregnant." Corinne didn't know why she said it. It wasn't in response to Martin's statement about marriage.

No, she hadn't married in the last four years. In fact, she had done many things she would rather not talk about in the times prior to her salvation in Jesus Christ.

Even though God had saved her from all her sins—past, present, and future—she was still saddled with the consequences of her past sins.

All color drained from Martin's face. "W-what?"

"Two months along. It was against my will, but

I'm keeping the baby." Corinne touched her tummy. "It's not the baby's fault."

Martin had to think for a moment. "You're married?"

"No. I'm not married."

"Ever?"

"Ever." Corinne drew a deep breath. "I'm not proud of my life before I became a Christian."

"Who is?" Martin replied.

Corinne made more gestures with her arms. In the sunlight, the plastic beads shone. She quickly retracted her arm.

When she looked at Martin, his eyes were on her wrist.

"Did your daughter make you that bracelet?" He asked quietly.

Corinne didn't reply.

She made a face as though Martin didn't understand her—and prayed that Flavian's men saw her—and repeated her directions. "You could turn left first and then make a right and walk down two blocks that way."

"You have two kids." Martin gasped.

"If you don't leave now, I will have none," Corinne whispered.

"What do you mean?"

A vehicle drove by slowly. Slam and Slime again.

Clearly they had been suspicious enough to leave their post and slow-drive past Corinne and Martin. Surely they knew who Martin was from that sidewalk encounter four nights before.

"Maybe you should stop at the visitor's center and get a map," Corinne said loudly.

As the SUV drove away, Corinne realized that Martin had taken a photo of it. "What are you doing?"

Martin didn't say.

"You better go," Corinne. "For both of our sakes."

"When do you get off work?"

Is he accepting me? Corinne couldn't possibly fathom anyone on earth wanting her after all that she had done and been through.

Only God had taken her in, cleansed off her sins and stains, and forgiven her soul forever.

"I can't." Corinne walked back to the bench, grabbed her lunch bag, and went back into the chocolate shop.

CHAPTER FIFTEEN

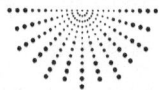

Inside the shop, Corinne went back to work. Every now and then, she glanced at the front door to make sure that Martin didn't walk in.

Or maybe to see if he would.

As the minutes and hours rolled by, Corinne lost hope that she would see Martin.

Oh well. Maybe I scared him off last Thursday when I fainted at the sight of him.

She chuckled.

"What's the inside joke?" Erika leaned toward her as she walked by with a tub of homemade ice cream.

Corinne didn't get a chance to answer her as more customers filed in.

Among them was...Nikos.

What is he doing here?

Corinne scanned the store to see if Sandra was around. The last thing Corinne wanted to do was cause trouble for Sandra. Corinne needed this job. A few more months, and she'd have enough to buy a car.

And then she would take Dahlia and run.

Nikos was accompanied by a few men in Hawaiian shirts, as if to blend in.

"Let's get a few pounds of fudge for our deep-sea fishing trip," Nikos said too loudly.

Corinne wondered if she should assume that Nikos was really going deep-sea fishing or whether he meant some other type of fishing.

"May I help you?" Erika put down the ice cream tub and looked at the customers.

Nikos pointed to Corinne. "Let her take care of me."

Erika opened her mouth to protest. "I can..."

Corinne stepped over, smiled to Erika, and sent her off to help other customers. When she turned back toward Nikos, she spotted the new hire—who had filled in for her on Sunday—helping other customers. Corinne tried to remember her name. Pamela or something.

"Do we get samples around here?" Nikos laughed.

"Yes, sir." Corinne showed them the array of fudge next to the ice cream bar. "Which would you like to try?"

"The sweetest ones are the most delicious," Nikos said.

The hair on Corinne's arms stood up, and she felt warm all of a sudden. The warmth of seething anger.

Forgive me, Lord. This man should be in jail.

In fact, both Flavian and Nikos should be in jail for what they did to me.

And yet Corinne could not think of how she was going to get justice.

Could she hire a private investigator?

Nope. No money.

All she could think of was running. Hiding.

For the rest of her life.

Nikos pointed to some dark chocolate fudge. "Let me try that first."

"It's dark chocolate and has the least sugar," Corinne said.

"But it's still sweet though?" His voice lowered. Somehow it sounded calmer.

Yeah, that was the thing that had kept Corinne alive.

Nikos might be crazy and did crazy things—like making her sit outside in the hot sun for fifteen minutes every day—but he still had a soft spot for her.

He wouldn't let anyone hurt Corinne because he wanted to do that himself.

And he had done it—not for Corinne's sake, but to get back at his former business partner who had stolen the diamonds from him.

As Corinne cut a small piece of the fudge for Nikos to try, she thought about how it could all go down.

At some point in time, Nikos and Flavian had to confront each other.

Corinne prayed that her children would not be in the crossfire.

Please, Lord. Save us. Spare us.

"You're right, Gail." Nikos chewed slowly. "It's not sweet enough. Give me something sweet."

Gail.

Corinne hope nobody else heard him.

Sometimes she wondered why she even bothered to use different names at different places. After all her trouble, Nikos had tracked her down to Key Largo.

Whether she went by Gail or Dinah, it made no difference.

All the men in her life had tracked her down.

Including Martin, who knew her by her real name.

Nikos's eyes were on her now, as if prying into her mind to read her thoughts. Corinne kept her breath even and tried not to think about all the things Nikos could do to her. His death threats, particularly.

Right now, though, Nikos could do nothing to her. It wasn't because she was in public or that it was daylight.

It was because Nikos knew Corinne could lead him to the South African diamonds that Flavian had stolen from him which had led to the fallout in the two men's business relationship.

Yes, for now, Corinne had the upper hand.

Corinne pointed to another block of fudge. "This one has maple syrup in it, plus pecans."

"I like maple syrup." Nikos's eyes brightened like a little boy's. "Gimme a sample of that, please."

When Nikos wasn't high on something, he could communicate like normal people.

Ditto with Flavian.

How on earth had she ended up with these two people, Corinne could never figure out. Somewhere at the back of her mind, she suspected that it might be the effects of sowing and reaping.

She sowed to a life of sin.

She reaped an environment of sin.

My soul is free now, even though I am still stuck in this physical prison.

"...five pounds." Nikos said.

"Each pound is $24.99," Corinne said. "Plus tax."

"Five pounds of the maple syrupy thingy with the pecans in it."

"Yes, sir." Corinne weighed five pounds of fudge and boxed it.

Nikos and his men followed Corinne to the register. Corinne rang it up.

Nikos gave her two hundred dollars. "Keep the change."

"You can put the tips in that jar over there." Corinne pointed to a glass jar filled with coins.

"You don't want my money?" Nikos asked.

Corinne didn't reply. She put the fudge box into a paper bag. Put the receipt in it. "Thank you, sir."

And don't come back.

CHAPTER SIXTEEN

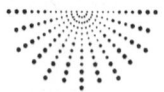

Martin stepped away from the chocolate shop window as soon as the four men inside turned away from the checkout register and walked toward the front door. He put away his phone just as he heard the door chime.

Not wanting to be seen, he slipped into the apparel store next door, and looked out the window.

The man with the short platinum blond hair and botched tattoos on the back of his arm didn't say a word to the man who opened the car door for him.

They drove away, but Martin had already taken a photo of the vehicle tag while the three men were in the chocolate shop.

Is Corinne okay?

Martin debated whether to go inside Key Largo Chocolate Shop and ask her. That meant he had to buy more chocolate or something.

Maybe some pralines.

Yeah.

But first, he'd better send those photos to Ming —wait. Ming said he would be unreachable. Martin had to send those photos to Pilar instead.

Okay. If Ming trusts her, I can too.

He sent the photos of the getaway vehicle— haha!—and the other grainy photos he had taken of the men while they were inside the shop.

They seemed to know Corinne.

She wasn't afraid of them.

Martin wondered if the blond man was the father of Corinne's unborn child.

"May I help you?" Someone said to him sweetly.

Martin realized he was still standing in the apparel shop. He had to come up with a reason for going into a store and then working on his phone instead of shopping.

He smiled. "Can't get away from work even when I'm on vacation."

She smiled.

"Yes, you might be able to help me." Martin put

away his phone for a second time in minutes. "I'm looking for a tee shirt for my dad. He wears XXL, but sometimes those things run small, you know?"

"We have large tee shirts here." The salesperson led Martin down a row of shirts and sweatshirts and ball caps.

"It has to be one hundred percent cotton. He won't wear anything else."

"Of course. We have all sorts of materials." She pointed. "Cotton here. Blended there."

"Thank you. And where are the women's sweatshirts? I'm looking for something for my sister too."

The girl pointed. "If there's anything else I can help you with, just let me know."

"I will. Thank you."

When she left Martin alone in a sea of pastel-colored shirts, Martin felt overwhelmed. He had never shopped for Dad. What would he wear? Tina would know, but Martin wasn't about to call her just to ask a simple question.

He decided to buy a tee shirt he himself liked. Maybe Dad would like it too. And if Dad didn't, Martin could wear it.

Ten minutes and six shirts later—three tee shirts for the summer and three sweatshirts for the mild Savannah winter—Martin walked out into the sunshine and to a text from Pilar. He sent her the photographs he had taken of the men and their car, with a short reply. "You're welcome."

Then he walked down to the ice-cream shop and bought a sorbet for the warm afternoon. Instead of walking up and down the main street like a typical tourist, he decided to find a bookstore to while away the entire afternoon.

What choice did he have?

The chocolate shop hadn't called him back about a job. He wondered if he should call the owner about it. On the other hand, if he worked there, it might complicate things. He might accidentally call Dinah by her real name.

Or something.

Across the busy street, and away from his car, Martin found an antiquarian bookstore with equally old chairs in it where he could sit down to read on his phone.

Unfortunately, the signal inside the old store was intermittent, and Martin found himself walking back outside.

I am really wasting time.

The sun baked the concrete pavement at ninety degrees this afternoon, and Martin knew he could not sit in his car in this sort of weather. His best bet was to return to the hotel.

On the one hand, there was little he could do in Key Largo. Even if he confronted Corinne again, there was no guarantee that she would be upfront with him and answer every question he had.

And he had many questions.

The most neutral ground he had found so far—maybe a safe space—was at church. However, church wasn't for another six days.

The next best thing that could happen was for Martin to get concrete news from Pilar. However, Pilar also might not share everything with him until her final report, whenever that was.

Martin walked back to his Shelby, feeling alone.

Just me and my car.

He turned on the air-conditioner at full blast, and started to drive south. Key West was only ninety-seven miles from here. Even if he drove slowly, he'd still get there in under three hours. That would take him to about four o'clock in the afternoon.

Maybe he could find a place to sit and stare at the ocean.

To think.

To pray.

And if there was any time left, he'd call his sister. He liked to hear Tina's voice. It reminded him of Mom's voice.

I miss Mom.

But we can't roll back the clock.

Martin realized then that he couldn't roll back time with Corinne either. Maybe their relationship was best left in the past. Maybe what they had four years ago was all there was to it.

On Sunday at church, Martin had found out that Corinne was the mother of a three-year-old.

On Monday, he found out she was pregnant again.

Two kids and unmarried.

He replayed their conversation at the bench at lunch time.

It was against my will, but I'm keeping the baby.

What did she mean? Had she been...

Martin couldn't bring himself to think the word, let alone say it aloud—although there was no one else in the car.

"Lord Jesus, I have no idea what Corinne is going through—or has gone through—but I pray that from this point forward, she would be in Your perfect will for her life. I hope that's a good prayer, Lord."

He stopped at a gas station to fill up the tank, and to get some cold bottles of water.

Then he drove in silence all the way to Key West.

CHAPTER SEVENTEEN

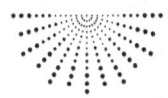

*B*y the time Corinne finished Erika's shift, it was nine o'clock at night. She worried about walking home in the dark, but she didn't want to spend money calling Uber.

Erika had a family emergency at the last minute, and Corinne felt obligated to fill in for her.

The new hire, Pilar, had offered to give her a ride. Although Corinne had seen her at church on Sunday, she was wary about trusting a stranger. Corinne didn't want Pilar to know where she lived.

Usually, if she had to work late, she would wait for Erika to get off work, so that she could get a ride home. Sometimes Erika stayed for a late dinner as her payment for the trouble. Most of the time, Erika didn't want Corinne to pay her back.

If Erika wasn't available, the owner's son usually was. Hardin was a nice boy, though Corinne had repeatedly turned down his invitation to go to the movies with him. Thing is, not only was he Sandra's son, he was also at least ten years younger than Corinne. She was sure Hardin wasn't ready for her problems.

Tonight, none of that mattered. Neither Erika nor Hardin was available.

Corinne would have to close up the shop and walk home.

The back parking lot was dark since one of the streetlights was broken. Corinne decided to leave from the front entrance instead.

The sidewalk was crowded with tourists. Corinne could hear bar music come from up and down the street on both sides of her. People talking, laughing. Cars honking, engines running.

The night air was warm, and Corinne wanted to take off her long-sleeved blouse. Nobody would see her bruises in the dark, she figured.

Her arm muscles were still sore every now and then, but the generic ointment she had bought at the pharmacy helped quite a bit. As soon as she reached Wanda's house, she would get into a hot tub. She'd feel better after that.

Crossing a corner, Corinne debated whether to take the short cut. She could be home in twenty minutes if she took the lane to her left. If she kept walking, there would be streetlights, but it would take her another fifteen minutes of navigating through more roads.

She hesitated.

Lord Jesus, which way should I go?

Against a bad feeling, Corinne turned left.

A few people walked unsteadily past her, smelling like booze. A couple of catcalls later, Corinne wanted to turn around and run back to the light.

But she didn't.

Her feet kept going.

Directly into the shadows.

Her phone rang, startling her. It was Erika, to Corinne's relief.

~

*B*eyond tired, Martin had arrived back in Key Largo just in time to see Pilar leave the backlot of the Key Largo Chocolate Shop.

Thanks to Martin's voluntary work this afternoon, Pilar had been able to send the license plate to her contacts. Obviously grateful, Pilar texted Martin—while he was sitting on a public beach in Key West—that Corinne was getting off work at nine o'clock tonight and had refused any ride home.

Something between the lines had told Martin that Pilar could use an extra set of eyes.

No, Martin had not had any special training, but he was bigger and more muscular than Pilar. He could, technically, be of assistance.

Somehow.

Two hours and a few minutes after that text message, Martin was back in Key Largo. He grabbed a quick takeout dinner somewhere in town, and ate in the car as he waited for Pilar to leave the shop.

He followed Pilar around.

Turned out that Pilar was waiting, just as he was.

Martin exchanged text messages with Pilar. He didn't find out much about Pilar, since he did most of the texting. However, he did find out that Pilar had grown up in Florida, and was a friend of one of the private investigators who worked for Ming's friend in Savannah. Hugo Something. He had been the person to introduce Ming to Pilar.

Pilar had been living in Miami for a few years,

trying to establish her own private investigation firm. Then she moved to Charleston to work security for a couple of years before returning to Miami. It had been in Charleston that she had met Ming, when she was working on an assignment for Hu Knows, Inc. Pilar and Ming kept in touch, even after she had moved home to Miami to care for her elderly parents.

Their conversation had ended when they saw Corinne lock the front door of the chocolate shop and started walking.

"Bad idea to walk alone, Corinne," Martin said aloud in his car.

In front of him, Pilar was in her charcoal SUV with a dent in the back fender. She was slowing down a bit. So did Martin.

At the street corner, Corinne climbed into a SUV.

Under the street light, Martin thought the driver looked like Erika from the chocolate shop.

Suddenly, a van pulled past Martin's car, sideswiped Pilar's SUV ahead of him, and rammed into Erika's vehicle.

Martin slammed on his brakes so he didn't plough into Pilar, who lost control of her vehicle, ramming it into a parked car.

Under the street lights, Pilar's airbag deployed.

Martin heard a couple of gunshots, and a woman screaming. Then he heard vehicle doors slam.

The van took off.

Martin pulled up behind Pilar's vehicle and called 911. He ran toward the driver's side and opened the door. Pilar reached out, and Martin helped her out of her SUV.

"Let's go!" Pilar shook all over. "You drive."

They scrambled back into Martin's car. He floored the gas pedal, and they were off.

"There! The van just turned down that street." Pilar pointed with a trembling hand.

She still seemed to be shaken up.

Watching her pull out a handgun freaked out Martin. "What are you doing?"

"Just drive." Her voice was calming down.

And drive, Martin did. He wished he hadn't painted his car bright tangerine. Now it was hard to hide in the night.

The van accelerated and so did Martin.

"I can't see the plates. Can you?" Pilar asked.

"I'm doing well not to lose control of my car." He could push ninety or maybe ninety-five miles per hour, but he had never gone beyond that on this poor old car, an original Shelby.

A bright light in his rearview mirror caught Martin's attention. "Someone's tailing us."

Pilar glanced back. "I wonder who."

The SUV didn't try to pass them. It came dangerously close to Martin—so close that he could see the passenger's face.

"Looks like the same guys from this afternoon." Martin kept his hands on the steering wheel.

He had told Pilar about the drive-by at lunch, and sent her the photograph of the license place he had taken.

"I'm still waiting for information," Pilar said.

"Don't let them see your gun. They might get trigger happy," Martin warned.

The SUV suddenly swerved toward Martin's car. He overcorrected and his Shelby screeched into the emergency lane. The SUV came at them again and rammed the side of Martin's car.

"Are they on our side?" Martin asked, flooring the accelerator.

"I don't know—"

The SUV hit the Shelby again, and this time Martin lost control of his car. One more push, and the car was in the ditch by the side of the road.

The airbags deployed.

"Not again!" Pilar's voice was muffled.

New lights appeared in Martin's rearview mirror. "What now?"

Blue flashing lights.

He heard some sort of whoop whoop sound.

Up ahead, the SUV and black van disappeared into the night.

Martin was too stunned to pray.

CHAPTER EIGHTEEN

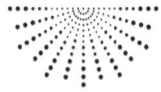

*A*fter giving their statements to the Monroe County Sheriff, Martin was allowed to leave the side of the road, but he waited for Pilar, who stayed behind to talk to the law enforcement personnel.

Martin figured it would be a long night for them.

He texted Pete to come get them since both his car and Pilar's SUV were out of commission. Pete gave him the number of a local tow truck and a mechanic in Miami who could repair his Shelby.

Martin didn't want to call Dad and worry him. Besides, it was a long way to haul his car back to Savannah. At the very least, Pete's friend could give him an estimate of the damage.

He didn't want to leave his key in the ignition, so he waited for the tow truck, who came about the same time as Pete.

Martin prayed that the police would find Corinne. And that, in the meantime, God would keep her safe.

He wasn't sure how he was going to handle it if he lost her a second time.

Pete took Martin and Pilar back to the hotel. It was convenient that both of them were staying in the same hotel.

After a quick shower, Martin couldn't sleep. He felt restless. He called Corinne's pastor from the phone number at the back of last Sunday's church bulletin, and told him everything that had happened that night, remembering as hard as he could that Corinne went by Dinah now.

Still, when he reverted back to calling her Corinne enough times, Pastor Butler caught on. "No wonder we know so little about her past."

"We'll sort out names later. Right now, I need to find out where Co—Dinah—lives. Her daughter could be in danger."

"And Wanda as well." Butler gave Martin his home address, and Martin called Uber.

The painted house was nestled among many other nondescript coastal-style houses up and down the road. The pastor was waiting outside his front door.

Pastor Butler climbed into the backseat with Martin. He buckled in.

"Wanda lives five minutes from here." Pastor Butler swiped his phone to get the address for the Uber driver.

"All we can do now is pray, really." Pastor Butler moved on to the most important call to action.

Martin was reminded again that there were more critical matters than his muscle car. In fact, if he had to sell his muscle car and his hard-earned share of the family business, he would—if he could get Corinne back.

It wouldn't be a fair trade, as Corinne was more precious than anything—or anyone else—in this world.

"I should have married her four years ago," Martin blurted as the car backed out of the pastor's driveway.

"We can't go back, but you knew that. We just have to trust that Almighty God has a better plan than ours." Pastor Butler turned up the sound on his phone so that Martin could hear the directions.

The driver drove within the speed limit, but Martin wished he could go faster.

"Sometimes God allows what He allows for a greater good."

Martin grunted. "Like what? Corinne's been through so much. I wasn't there to protect her."

"You are now."

"Am I? We lost her tonight."

"Have you?"

"I don't know."

"Exactly, Martin. Only God knows."

"You're saying..."

"Let this play out. We'll see where it goes. We pray all the way that God will keep Corinne safe. She is praying too."

Before they arrived, the entire street had been blocked off by police cars and fire trucks. Martin had no idea Key Largo had this many cops in town.

Before the Uber driver could find a place by the side of the road to let them off, a police officer stopped his car and approached the driver side. "No parking, sir. You'll have to take another road."

"We're here to see Wanda Lewis," Pastor Butler said from the backseat. "I'm Wanda's pastor from her church."

The officer paused for a second. "I'm sorry, Pastor. Miss Lewis is dead."

Martin couldn't breathe. "What about Corinne's daughter, Dahlia?"

The office raised his eyebrows.

Martin suspected they had no idea anyone else was supposed to be in the house. He figured that after Corinne's abduction, the Key Largo police went to her house and found Wanda dead.

Surely they could tell if there had been a child in the house. For example, when Martin went to see his sister Tina in Atlanta, her house was strewn with children's toys and clothes.

If, in fact, the police could not tell that Dahlia had been in the house, it could mean that Corinne had been prepared to run.

Again.

"Dahlia is only three years old," Martin added, trying to be helpful. "And Corinne's pregnant."

"Due in seven months." Pastor Butler let out a grunt of some sort.

In seven months? Who's the father? Martin played back his meeting with Corinne at the sidewalk bench, followed by the visitors to the chocolate shop. He wondered if he should tell the police about Corinne's visitors, but he had sent those photos to Pilar, who had in turn sent them off to people she knew.

Martin had to find some way to help Corinne. He felt alone.

Please, God, let her live.

The officer kept his poker face, but Martin was sure he had provided the police with new information that they would have to process.

Martin turned to the Uber driver. "Could you wait for us?"

"It's going to cost you," he said.

"No problem. Read a book." Martin smiled. "Thanks, man."

As the officer led Martin and Pastor Butler to Wanda's house, Martin saw the sidewalk stranger again. This time, she had a badge of some sort dangling over her belt.

She looked straight at Martin.

And Martin flinched.

~

She walked toward Martin.

Martin stepped back before he realized how dumb that was. He stepped forward again, but it was too late.

A little smile escaped her face. "FBI Special Agent Ruby Tanaka."

At this point, Martin figured he had two options: reply in kind or play hostile witness.

He had never met an FBI agent before—

Well, I'll take that back. Camden La Salle from Riverside Chapel still works for the FBI.

Martin extended his hand, but Tanaka didn't shake it.

"I'm wearing examination gloves," she said.

"Oh. Germs?"

"I don't know what she sees in you." Tanaka shook her head.

"You know who I am."

"Your arrival in Key Largo is interfering with an ongoing operation." Tanaka stared at him in the dim street lights above them on the cracked sidewalk.

Ongoing operation? What is Corinne knee-deep in? "I'm sorry. Is there anything I can do?"

"What can a long-lost boyfriend from another life do?"

Martin wondered if it was a rhetorical question or an insult.

"You and that private investigator." Tanaka frowned. "Interfering."

"I'm sorry for both of us. It's my fault. I was the one who wanted to find Corinne."

Tanaka didn't correct him. To Martin, it meant that she knew Corinne was Dinah.

A sudden realization hit Martin. "Please don't

tell me I brought evil into town, that Corinne was abducted because of me."

"Evil?" Tanaka tilted her head. "If you must know, it was already here. You walked into a viper's nest."

"God, please forgive me." Martin closed his eyes. When he opened his eyes, Tanaka was walking away. Martin went after her. "Wait! Wait!"

Tanaka stopped.

"Aren't you going to ask me questions?" Martin asked.

"What questions might I ask you?"

"I don't know. I took those photos this afternoon that Pilar sent to your office."

"I already know that."

"Maybe if you ask me questions, I might prove useful."

"You're desperate to help."

"Yes, ma'am."

"Then go home to Savannah, Mr. MacFarland. If Dinah wants to see you, she will visit you. Don't try to look for her again."

In other words, stay away.

There was no way Martin could stay still. His mind churned through several ideas. He thought he might call Ming again for help. Then again, wasn't Ming unavailable all week?

Tanaka turned and walked back to the crime scene, passing by Pastor Butler coming toward Martin.

"Let's go home," Butler said. "Then you go back to your hotel to get some sleep. We'll talk in the morning."

"Is there any more we can do right now?" Martin walked with him to the car. When the Uber driver saw them coming, he put away his phone.

"I have to tell Pete that Wanda is dead," Butler replied. "He would want to know right away."

Martin's watch said it was past midnight. "Won't he be asleep?"

"Pete was going to ask Wanda to go out with him."

"But he never got around to it," Martin finished for him.

He didn't know Pete from Adam, and he might be projecting his own failures on Pete. If he had somehow not lost Corinne four years before, none of this mess would have happened today.

Martin got into the passenger side. "I won't be able to sleep tonight anyway. If you want us to go to Pete's house, we could do that." He turned to the Uber driver. "Yes?"

"At your service, sir." The driver turned on the ignition.

"All right. Let's go." Butler got into the back-seat. "I have to call my wife. She leads the Women's Prayer Team, and they'd want to know too."

"We need all the prayer we can get." Martin held back his tears. "I just want Corinne and her daughter home safely."

"That's our priority prayer."

CHAPTER NINETEEN

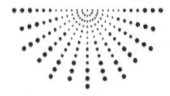

*C*orinne didn't know how long she had been in the van, since she passed out when they took her away. They kept her wrists tied up behind her, and she was lying down on some musty-smelling sleeping bag. No pillow. No safety belts.

She finally woke up, thanks to the motion of the vehicle on bumpy roads. If she were to guess, she would say the road was probably not paved.

Her sense of time went out the window, and she closed her eyes to pray and rest. She would need all the strength and energy to get out of this.

With God's power.

The two men in the driver's and passenger seats didn't talk to each other at all while Corinne was awake. She knew who they were, knew they worked for Nikos.

But why would Nikos abduct the mother of his unborn child?

Probably to get back at Flavian.

How Corinne hated to be in the middle of the crossfire between these two sworn enemies.

For the longest time, the FBI had tried to gather enough evidence against Flavian for his hand in money laundering activities for some criminal organization. It had turned out that the FBI only wanted to use Flavian as a stepping stone to some international terrorist.

After failing to make anyone turn against Flavian, the FBI got to Corinne.

As a mother of Dahlia—then only a year old and being weaned—Corinne had to do what was best for her.

Was Dahlia going to have a decent life living in the shadows of a father who had broken so many laws that he'd go to jail for a very long time—if caught?

All Corinne did for Flavian was bookkeeping.

Well, and dating him.

When the FBI special agent showed Corinne how awful that terrorist was, and how Flavian was responsible for converting stolen diamonds into money for arms in the black market, Corinne had enough. The agent said that the Department of Treasury was interested in the money laundering aspect of it, while the FBI wanted to go after the terrorist.

Once Corinne agreed to help, she suddenly had a fully grown best friend from college named Stephanie, who showed up at the Hawaiian vacation resort one day, and showed her more photos of Flavian in bed with the terrorist, a woman they called Molyneux.

That was all it took to turn Corinne. Flavian was sleeping around. He was never going to marry her.

After that mother-and-daughter vacation in Hawaii, Corinne did everything she could to help Stephanie, whom Corinne suspected was from the FBI. Months later, she had her opportunity when she memorized the combination to Flavian's private safe.

She took the pouch of diamonds from Flavian's private safe in his mansion, put Dahlia in the car seat, and some clothes in the trunk, left the diamonds in a drop box.

And vanished from Flavian's life.

The same way she had vanished from Martin's life four years before.

Within the next six weeks, the FBI had given Corinne a new identity and a new start in sunny Florida, where she never expected to see Flavian or Nikos again.

Or Martin, for that matter.

Martin. Oh Martin.

A drop of tear trickled down the side of her face.

Why did you come to Key Largo, Martin?

Nothing good can come of this.

Now Corinne heard noise, like a garage door opening. The van slowed down, rolled forward, then stopped altogether.

The door opened.

"Let's go." It was a different person now. A woman, this time.

Corinne didn't know whether that made any difference. She could take out that small petite woman if she wanted to, but not with both hands tied behind her back.

Besides, she didn't want to hurt the baby in her belly.

Surely, Nikos had considered that too.

Corinne sat up as best she could, and scooted toward the door. The woman helped her out of the van onto the garage floor. The air was dusty and muggy, so they must still be in

Florida somewhere. Or Alabama. Or South
Georgia.

"How was your ride?" The woman didn't smile.
The perfunctory politeness ran counter to the
flame of anger in her eyes.

"Long and bumpy," Corinne said softly.

"Long? It's only an hour and a half."

"Oh? I thought I've been in the van for hours."

"Darkness does that to you." Then she
clammed up.

An hour and a half. Where could they go in
that amount of time? Key West to the south. Miami
or Miami Beach to the north.

The woman didn't give Corinne more time to
think. She grasped her arm and led her across the
garage floor to another van. There were several
people at stations here and there. Corinne had
never seen them before.

"Where are we going?" Corinne walked slowly,
to give herself time to recover and think.

The woman did not reply.

"Who are you?" Corinne asked.

No answer either.

Corinne stopped at the van.

"Get in," the woman said.

This time, Corinne decided enough was
enough. "No."

"Get in!" The woman's voice turned harsh.

"Not until you tell me where we're going."

The woman motioned for a couple of people to come over. "We were going to do this when you're on the boat, but this is fine too."

"Boat? Where are we going?" Corinne felt a quick pinch on her upper arm.

And then her world faded to black.

~

*S*omewhere on the boat between the night sky and certain death, Corinne woke up to the smell of fuel and noisy engine. She found her hands tied behind her. She rolled over and tried to sit up.

Someone helped her up.

It was the same woman. Must be Corinne's new handler.

Another handler.

In the last four years she had somehow found herself in the position of requiring handlers. First, it was a bodyguard—or so Flavian had called him— who followed her everywhere she went. That first FBI handler lasted for one year, until he was reassigned.

Then Corinne was passed on to her second FBI

handler. After handing the bag of diamonds to her and telling her about the assault, Corinne found her reprieve and retired from answering to anyone but God. She was happy that the FBI let her go. The US Marshals met her at an undisclosed location, and whisked her away across the country to a new place, a new identity, and a new life for her and her daughter.

Key Largo had been a hiding place for her.

Until now.

Only God can help me now.

The boat docked in the dark of night.

The woman with no name helped Corinne out of the boat. A small van came to get them.

Corinne felt carsick. She closed her eyes. Felt like throwing up.

Somehow the minutes passed, and the van dropped them off in some building that Corinne could not see.

The hallway was dark. Grime everywhere. Like it was part of a workshop or at the back of a building. Or someplace like that.

Corinne coughed softly at the dust.

The woman didn't say a word.

She tightened her grip on Corinne's arm as she helped her take the short steps up to another door, heavily guarded this time by armed men.

Pushing Corinne in, the woman followed with a serrated blade.

Corinne gasped.

"Turn around," the woman ordered.

Corinne had no choice. She was facing a stark white wall. There was a steel single bed pushed up against the wall. Nothing else in the room. No table. No chair.

But then she felt her wrists go free. She massaged her wrists. "Thank you."

"Thank you?" The woman's eyebrows rose. "You're thanking me?"

Corinne didn't know how to respond, except to ask for her name.

"You can call me your executioner." She laughed. "We're not friends. You took my man. You took my future. I will take your life."

"What life did I have with Flavian?" Corinne had no idea who this woman was.

Miss Executioner didn't answer. She marched out of the room and slammed the door behind her.

Corinne heard the key turn on the other side.

Executioner.

Stunned, Corinne's knees went weak.

CHAPTER TWENTY

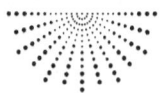

When Martin knocked on Pilar's hotel room, no one replied. Of course, her SUV wasn't parked outside because it had been towed the night before from downtown Key Largo—if the little peninsula had any downtown at all.

He knocked again.

He didn't hear anything.

Martin called Pilar's phone. No reply.

He knocked again.

"All right! All right!" Pilar's voice was muffled.

Martin waited. When the door opened, he was shocked. "You look awful."

Her face was bruised, and so were her arms.

"That's what I get for being petite and smaller than the airbag. What do you want?"

"Any leads?"

"Are you an investigator?"

"Just a concerned friend of the abductee."

"Abductee?" Pilar groaned as she stepped aside. "Come on in."

Before Pilar could say anything, Martin blurted, "I want to help."

"You can pray." Pilar closed the laptop on the round table—the only table—in the small hotel room.

"That too, but give me something to do." Martin looked intently at Pilar, to show her that he was genuine.

"You have no training." Pilar opened a small refrigerator below a television set. "Want some water?"

"No, but have you eaten breakfast?"

"Are you taking me to breakfast?" Pilar pointed to her face. "I can't go out like this. Someone is going to say you beat me up."

Martin didn't think it was funny. "Breakfast on me if you let me help."

"I'm not hungry, and no, I don't want you to get shot at or something." Pilar grinned. "Then what do I say to Ming?"

"That I volunteered." Martin spread his hands to show he was sincere. "Look, Pilar. You have no assistants. You work alone. You are it at your PI firm. Ming is too far away to get here. Every minute we waste, Corinne might be another minute closer to death. Not only her, but her daughter as well."

"And she still doesn't want you back."

"I don't care about that right now. As long as Corinne and her daughter are safe, I can rest easy the rest of my life."

Pilar drank more water.

"In fact, while I know that God has allowed me to come here to see Corinne, I don't know what's next for us. It might be that this is the closure He is giving me and nothing more."

Pilar nodded.

"Sometimes we grow up and move on, and maybe Corinne and I—our relationship—are past history. Maybe she's not in my future and I'm not in hers. As long as she lives, I'm happy to go home and leave her be." Martin paused. "After we make sure she's safe."

Pilar tossed the empty bottle of water into a trash can. "Sit down."

hy can't we trust the FBI?

The question gnawed at Martin long after he had left Pilar's hotel room. He called Pete right after his meeting with Pilar.

Pete didn't want to talk over the phone for some reason. Instead, he invited Martin to meet with him —not at his house, but at Angelina's houseboat.

Martin wasn't allowed to drive his bright tangerine Shelby.

And no Uber or Lyft either.

Martin took a cab to the corner of Overseas Highway and Sunset Boulevard. Fifteen minutes later, a little gray Toyota showed up to pick him up.

The driver was wearing a hat and large sunglasses covered half her face. Her nails were painted bright red.

"Hello, Angelina." Martin smiled as he fastened his seat belt.

"How did you know it was me?" Angelina sighed.

"I guessed."

Angelina didn't answer her. "Did you know I used to work as a dispatcher?"

"You did? I had no idea. Thank you for your service." Martin didn't know what else to say.

"I did what I could since I flunked out of the police academy."

"It's a difficult job."

"I tried."

"I'm sure you did."

"Three times." Angelina drove within speed limits and turned on her blinker long before she made a turn into any street. "After that, I took it as a sign from God that I wasn't cut out to be a police officer even though that has always been my dream."

"Why are you telling me all this?" Martin wasn't sure he wanted to know the answer.

"Because I didn't want you to think I wasn't qualified to help you and Pete find Dinah and Dahlia."

"It never crossed my mind." What crossed his mind was his own thoughts that Pilar found him lacking.

No matter.

Pete had offered to help. Martin accepted it without knowing what Pete could or could not do.

Martin had kept the original photographs of the SUV vehicle tag and the men who visited Corinne before she was abducted. All that might lead to something, right?

Maybe if he and Pete put their heads together...

"I'm assuming that since Pete asked you to pick me up, that he had briefed you on what's happening," Martin said.

Angelina nodded. "I don't know how much I can help. It's been a while since I was a dispatcher, but I would have you know that I kept up with my other skills."

"What other skills?"

"I guess Pete didn't tell you."

"Tell me what?"

Angelina smiled. "Is spaghetti for lunch okay with you?"

"Lunch?" Martin glanced at his watch. It was only nine o'clock in the morning.

It felt like he had been up for hours.

Martin recalled his fruitless meeting with Pilar.

If the private investigator didn't need his help, what could his Three Stooges do? He felt that maybe he should give up organizing this ragtag team.

After all, he was only a private citizen. He didn't even know how to hold, let alone shoot, a gun.

Gun?

He was hoping to free Corinne with words. Negotiate her out of there.

Well, first, they had to find out where she was.

CHAPTER TWENTY-ONE

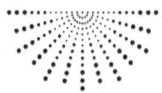

*B*y the second day, Corinne settled into a routine. The first thing they had brought her the last two mornings was breakfast. It consisted of stale cereal and watery milk.

Corinne said a blessing over her food before she ate. She held back her tears. She had to be strong to pray through this valley of the shadow of death.

Sunlight came in through the small square window toward the ceiling of her cell. It was too high up there for her to see through it. Otherwise she'd be curious about where they were.

She recalled the boat ride two nights before, but she had been half-unconscious. Since then, she hadn't left this cell of a room.

Are we on an island?

She didn't recall Flavian ever talking about any island other than Hawaii and...

Cuba.

Unless, of course, she had been out longer than she thought.

The bracelet on her wrist was gone. She wasn't sure when they had taken it away from her, but she hoped that the FBI had some leads. The GPS in her bracelet hadn't been turned on in a year, but she prayed that it still worked.

She prayed for Dahlia, whom she assumed was still back home in Key Largo with Wanda. She hoped that Wanda was doing okay taking care of Dahlia while Corinne was busy being abducted.

She prayed for Miss Executioner and her life problems.

She prayed for her abductor, which she assumed to be Flavian. Who else could it be?

After she finished breakfast, Corinne sang hymns to while away the time. Feeling exhausted for some reason, she nodded off.

She awoke again when Miss Executioner came into the room.

"I'm surprised you didn't try to escape," she said. "Then again, we're on an island."

Island.

"I'm enjoying my vacation." Corinne smiled. "Will there be a guided tour?"

"For you, a guided torment." Miss Executioner left the room again.

Why is she like that?

Maybe she needs Jesus.

Corinne prayed for her again.

~

*T*he bright and happy sounds of Dahlia laughing drained the blood from Corinne's face. She stopped short of entering the room, her feet cemented to the floor of the hallway, her palms sweating.

Dahlia.

I must be hearing things.

"Move!" Miss Executioner pushed the door and Corinne at the same time, nearly smacking Corinne's nose into the wooden door.

There, in the middle of some rays of sunlight streaming into the sitting room, was Corinne's daughter, playing with a dollhouse taller than she was. On a nearby sofa, Nikos was grinning broadly.

Nikos.

So it wasn't Flavian at all.

Corinne was sure it was Flavian who'd want his daughter back.

Not Nikos. He didn't care for anyone but himself.

Corinne was sure he didn't care for his baby in her womb either.

"Mommy!" Dahlia dropped a miniature piece of furniture and ran toward Corinne.

Corinne noticed a rhinestone-studded belt around her pajama top. "What are you wearing, baby?"

"A belt, Mommy. Christmas present from Unca Niko. So shiny, Mommy."

Christmas in June?

"What's this, Nikos?" Corinne felt the thick belt. It was metallic.

"Fifty thousand volts." Nikos smiled. "Maybe more."

"No! She's only a child!" Corinne hugged Dahlia, never wanting to let her go. Her eyes scanned the room. Security was everywhere.

"Look what else Unca Niko bought me!" Dahlia pointed at the dollhouse. "Come see it, Mommy!"

"Yes, come over and see this expensive toy I bought your daughter." Nikos patted the seat next to him.

Corinne ignored him. It was best to do so. Back in the days when Nikos and Flavian had been business partners at the casino—before the money laundering mess—Nikos had often visited Flavian and the then-pregnant Corinne.

In fact, it had been Nikos who introduced Flavian to his string of other girlfriends. Once Flavian picked his girls, Nikos would ruin them afterwards.

Corinne was done with Flavian and his business associates. She hoped never to see Flavian again. However, when she looked in her daughter's eyes, she could see traces of him.

Why did I mess up so badly, Lord?

She wondered what was going on and how she was going to get out of this predicament.

"Come over here and let me rub your belly to see how Flavian's baby is doing in there." Nikos jiggled a finger.

The gesture made Corinne feel sick. Her legs felt wobbly. She sank to the floor near the doll house, far enough away from Nikos.

Not Flavian's baby.

Corinne wasn't sure if she should correct Nikos about the baby's paternity.

"After we play family, you're going to Oscar and get my diamonds for me." Nikos smiled.

"You want me to leave the island?"

"That's the idea, woman." Nikos laughed. "We know where Oscar is. Go see him. I get my diamonds, you get your daughter back."

"You know that Oscar is Flavian's friend, not mine."

Nikos flicked a photograph at Corinne. It floated her way and fluttered to the floor. Corinne looked down.

Flavian. All beaten up. He looked barely alive.

"What happened to your boyfriend will happen to you too," Nikos grunted.

Ex-boyfriend.

Again, Corinne didn't know if she should correct Nikos.

"Is he dead?"Corinne asked instead.

"In the process."

"Let me see him. He knows Oscar."

"So do you."

"Not as well as he does."

"He can't travel right now. You can."

"Travel? To where?"

"Cuba, of course."

The last thing Corinne wanted was to leave her three-year-old in the hands of this criminal.

"You've always wanted everyone else's stuff," Corinne said. "You wanted Flavian's girls. His business, clients, money, diamonds. Everything. Coveting is a sin."

Nikos looked amused. "I thought you were attending a church in Key Largo for therapy. Now you're turning all holier-than-thou on me. What would Flavian say—well, he's not going to say much."

Corinne composed herself. "What did you do to Flavian? He's like a brother to you. He rescued you when you were a homeless kid."

"Well, he taught me well."

"How do I know he's not dead in this picture?" Corinne lifted the photo. "Let me see him."

"And you will get the diamonds for me?"

There, she caught him.

By not negating what she had said, Nikos showed his hand. He did have Flavian held somewhere.

"Where is Flavian?" Corinne asked.

"Bring me the diamonds, and I will let you see him."

"I have no idea where the diamonds are, but Oscar knows, right?" She was guessing. "You want me to call Oscar? Then give me something to say to him. A word from Flavian would go for miles."

"How do I know you don't have it stashed somewhere?" Nikos asked.

"Your suspicion is unfounded. I don't have Flavian's diamonds." She lifted her hands. "No ring. No jewelry. No diamonds."

It was the truth.

Corinne had kept nothing for herself.

Nonetheless, they were not technically Flavian's diamonds. Somehow stolen in one way or another, the diamonds made their way to Flavian's possession. His job was to get them to Oscar for distribution.

Nikos's eyes went to Dahlia, still playing. "Get me the diamonds, and Dahlia will be safe."

Corinne's eyes flared. "Let me speak with Flavian. If anyone could get us to Oscar, it's him."

"Us? You said *us*." Nikos looked at Dahlia, still playing in her toy kitchen. "I've always wanted a family."

Dahlia showed him a tiny little frying pan. Nikos pretended to eat out of it.

"No, no." Dahlia laughed. "Use a spoon!"

Nikos laughed.

Corinne cringed.

My poor little girl has no idea what was going on.

Nikos waved to a security guard. "Take her away."

"To see Flavian?" Corinne asked.

Nikos laughed. "No, of course not. Am I stupid? If I let you two meet, you'd plot against me, as you two have done for years."

"Years? I saw you for the first time only three years ago."

"Semantics." Nikos waved his arms. He left the sofa, kicked off his loafers, and joined Dahlia on the floor. "We can stay here as long as you want. But let's not take all day, shall we? I might change my mind about Dahlia."

It took all the willpower Corinne had not to lunge forward and push Nikos away from her daughter.

Help me. I want to kill him.

But she didn't. The guard escorted her out of the room.

As she was leaving, she heard Nikos's words. "Send Oscar my greetings!"

CHAPTER TWENTY-TWO

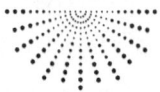

The weather turned. A squall was spotted out at sea. Then the thunderstorm came. Nikos called off the excursion to Cuba, saying that he wasn't going to risk his yacht in such weather.

Corinne asked again, and this time Nikos said she could see Flavian for ten minutes.

Miss Executioner came to get Corinne from her room. They walked one floor down. Corinne didn't freak out in the darkest hallway she had ever been in. She knew every step forward would perhaps lead to freedom.

When they reached one of the metal doors, Miss Executioner waved her magic key card. The door unlocked.

"Five minutes conjugal visit," Miss Executioner said.

"We're not married, and Nikos said ten."

Miss Executioner rolled her eyes. Corinne knew than that she wouldn't go against Nikos.

The door opened, and Corinne saw a man lying prone on the floor. He lifted his head, and she recognized him.

Just like the photograph, Flavian's face was black and blue. His clothes were torn and caked with blood.

"Gail?" Flavian sat up. One hand dangled.

"What did they do to you?" Corinne stepped in.

Behind them, Miss Executioner said, "Only to soften him up."

"It didn't work!" Flavian laughed.

He offered her a seat next to him. They sat on the floor, shoulder to shoulder. Oddly enough, Corinne didn't feel anything for him.

In all practicality, their relationship was over.

"I went to Key Largo to see you," Flavian said. "I didn't make it. I landed in Miami, and Nikos carjacked me."

"How did he know your schedule?"

Flavian shrugged. "Beats me. Only Slam and Slime knew where I was going."

"You still trust them?" Corinne asked, but Flavian didn't answer.

"Is Dahlia safe?"

Corinne shook her head and began to cry. "She's upstairs. Nikos bought her a kitchen play set."

Flavian seemed furious that Nikos had abducted his daughter and ex-girlfriend, but there was nothing he could do.

Flavian leaned toward her.

"There are usually two guards in this wing, plus Harper," he whispered.

"Harper?"

"The woman who always wears black."

"Miss Executioner."

"What?" Flavian chuckled softly.

"She has some sort of vendetta against me."

"You think you can help me take her out?" Flavian asked.

"Me?"

"Yeah. Don't tell me I wasted a lot of money sending you to self-defense class. And firearms class. And whatever other training I sent you to."

"I don't know..."

He hushed her. "Don't say you don't know. Say you will at least try."

Corinne didn't reply.

"When the guard opens the door to let you out, we'll take down Harper and we'll get out of here."

"Do you know the layout of the building?" Corinne asked.

Flavian nodded. "Four floors. We're in the base-ment, where there are about eight cells. This is our Alcatraz."

"I'm not on this floor, I don't think. They put me in another room."

"This cell here is facing east. I can tell from the morning sunlight."

"Okay." It might be useful later, Corinne figured. Or not. Right now the little slit of window was dark. Probably from the heavy rain.

"I just get sunlight. I don't know where they put me."

"Looks like a room?"

Corinne nodded. "Yeah, a regular empty room."

"Then it's one floor up."

"You know this place."

"I've been here exactly twice," Flavian said. "With Nikos, no less."

"Maybe he bought the island."

"Rent is more like it. He's too broke to buy

one." Flavian's eyes steeled. "Don't tell him anything."

"He wants your diamonds."

"You gave half of them to your cousin Stephanie, didn't you?" His eyes showed Corinne that he knew.

"I was under duress." Corinne didn't explain what sort of duress. It wasn't from the FBI, for sure. She couldn't raise a child in the dark world that Flavian operated in.

"I forgive you. You did it for our daughter. We should've left Vegas. You like Miami? When this is over, we can move to Miami."

Even as he said it, Corinne knew he could make no promises to leave his life of crime.

The door opened before they could talk more. Corinne had no idea what Flavian wanted her to do, but she didn't want to jeopardize Dahlia's safety. Yet, before she could leave the cell peacefully, Flavian was already attacking the guard.

Corinne rushed forward, but a muzzle pointed at her nose.

Miss Executioner shook her head. "Were you two thinking of fighting your way out?"

She nodded to the guard, who immediately tasered Flavian. The latter writhed in pain on the dirty floor.

"Flavian!" Corinne screamed. "No!"

Miss Executioner dragged Corinne out of the cell. Her last words to the guard were, "Break his legs."

CHAPTER TWENTY-THREE

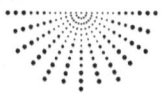

The Key West nightclub was neon loud in every way, psychedelic glow-in-the-dark colors splattered all over the walls and ceilings, and swirls of fluorescent paint on the bar, booths, and surrounding tables.

It was too noisy for Martin, but he pressed on, pushing deeper into the crowd reeking with the smell of liquor concoctions and cigarette smoke.

Suffocating!

Martin popped out of the dance crowd on the other side. He glanced around to gain his bearings and to see if he could remember his way out of here.

He looked at every face but did not see Pilar. The lighting had turned everyone's clothes another color, and Martin suddenly couldn't remember what Pilar had worn when she stepped off the van still parked outside.

He thought back to the last sixty hours he had spent with Pete and Angelina. It had turned out that in their spare time—back in the days—Pete and Angelina had been two small-town private investigators. They had retired from it twenty or more years ago after they had a falling out with each other.

Since they liked the beach so much, they both had refused to leave Key Largo. After their spouses had died, they patched up their differences.

Now they were called back to action again.

It took two days for the trio to track down the SUV that carried the two hunky men who ran Martin's car off the road on Monday night. Perhaps two days were a feat to some, but to Martin, it felt like forever.

Nevertheless, here they were.

The SUV had a stolen tag.

Tracking the story with their Private Investigator hats, Pete and Angelina scoured news reports until they found an interview with the original owner who had a security camera in his garage that recorded the theft.

The police sketch of the man looked like one of the two men in the SUV.

On Wednesday, Pete dusted off his old PI business card, drove up to Miami, and found the owner of the car whose tag had been stolen. Pete found out that the man knew the thieves. He had reported them to the police because they wouldn't pay him squat for something else.

Pete paid him whatever he needed—out of Martin's bank—and the dude talked like a parakeet.

Pete returned to Key Largo triumphant and loaded with new information, such as the name of the two men. It had turned out that when the two men came to Key Largo to find Dahlia—whom they knew as Gail—they had recruited a third man, then dumped him on the wayside once they had what they wanted from him.

When Martin found out what Pete had discovered, he swallowed his pride and called Pilar again, adding a condition that his team would be involved.

Thursday night came, and Pilar let Martin, Pete, and Angelina sit in the back of her rental van, while she went inside the Coconut Sunset Club.

Unfortunately, two hours later, Pilar did not emerge.

Martin decided he would go in. He found

himself wandering—or trying to—down a dark hallway.

"Off limits, sir." A burly man twice Martin's height said.

Well, okay, he wasn't exactly *twice* Martin's height, but he must be at least six foot seven. However, he was twice Martin's width. His arms were huge—

"You cannot come in here."

"Sorry, I'm..."

"What are you looking for?" Mr. Burly asked again.

"He's looking for me," a sweet voice said behind Martin.

He turned to find himself staring up at a woman with a face painted like a mask. She was smiling through thick lips and even thicker eyelashes. Her sequined dress sparkled as she changed position from one stiletto heel to the other.

She dipped her head down at Martin. Eyed him with a "you poor thing" look. Not one of disdain, but more a pity that he had to be here at all, outside his elements.

Or something like that.

Martin felt rather small with all these tall people around him, as though he had turned into a short elf all of a sudden.

The woman put a palm out. "Let's have it."

"How do I know you're the one?" Martin asked.

She laughed. Then placed a hand on Martin where no one other than his wife should—

"Stop it." Martin clenched his fingers and walked away.

He couldn't get through the crowd of dancers. He tried walking around them, but the tables were full now. Someone spilled drinks on his shirt.

"Hey, watch it!" It was the same woman, who had apparently followed him.

Martin was flicking liquid off his shirt with his free hand, but it had absorbed through to his chest. There was a piece of lemon sitting on top of his hip pack.

"Here, let me help you." The woman started to wipe his shirt with a cloth napkin.

Martin jumped back, playing the part. "No, no!"

"No, no?" She laughed. "I'm not a dog."

"No, no, no!" Martin placed both hands on the hip pack.

"Everything okay here?" Another woman's voice said, close to Martin's ears.

Martin made eye contact—

Agent Tanaka?

In a retro pink wig and black leather from head to toe.

"Who are you?" The woman with Martin asked Tanaka.

"Name's Free. Fancy Free." Tanaka turned to Martin. "What's your name, handsome?"

"Nobody." Two can play the part.

"Well, Mr. Nobody, let's finish this, shall we?" She strong-armed him, and led him back toward the hallway Martin had come from.

The other woman was left standing there.

Or so Martin thought.

Until he felt a prick in his neck—

CHAPTER TWENTY-FOUR

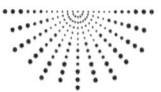

artin opened his eyes to a dark room and a stench that reminded him of sewage, to put it mildly. "What is this place?"

"The dungeon," a raspy voice answered.

Martin flinched. He realized he was lying prone on a concrete floor. "Am I hearing things?"

"I'm here."

Martin froze. Then: "Who?"

"Your fellow prisoner."

"Prison?" Martin rolled over and tried to sit up. He supposed he could play along. If he was stuck in this room with another *prisoner*, the last thing he'd want to do was make an enemy out of his cellmate.

"What are you in for?" Martin asked.

"Women problems."

"Ha." Maybe that dude had been in here too long. "What's your name?"

"Flavian."

"No last name?"

"Not to you. What's your name?"

"Martin."

"Martin?" His fellow prisoner cursed and started to yell. "That twisted Nikos puts two exes in the same cell."

"What? What exes?"

"Gail." The answer was almost a whisper, but Martin heard it.

Gail, also known as Dinah, also known as Corinne?

"You're Dahlia's dad." Martin still couldn't piece the whole puzzle together, but that much, he could guess.

"Yes. And you're the old boyfriend from back east, the reason Gail wouldn't marry me." There was no bitterness in Flavian's voice, as if he had resigned to his place.

"What?" Martin didn't want to presume anything beyond his own thoughts.

"She said she can't commit. Then she ghosted me." Flavian laughed.

"She ghosted me too," Martin said before he realized he might have spoken too much.

"But we both found her."

"Presumably."

"Ah, a philosopher in our midst."

"She might run again," Martin explained.

"Not from this island, she can't. Nikos will make sure of it."

"We have to get out of here." Martin touched the floor around him to see if he could find a wall. There was gunk on the floor. He wiped his palm on his pants and decided to wait until morning to *explore*. "What does Nikos want?"

"My diamonds. My business. My family. My daughter."

"Diamonds?" This story was getting more bizarre day after day to Martin.

"You shouldn't have gone to Key Largo. Why couldn't you let her be?" Flavian's voice tapered off. It seemed like he wanted to be angry with Martin, but he'd rather have the company.

"You said Key Largo. You knew where she is." Martin assumed they were both talking about the same woman.

Flavian didn't answer him.

"Tweedle Dee and Tweedle Dum. Your men?" Martin asked.

"Who?"

"Two big guys. Not quite sumo wrestlers."

"Ah. Slam and Slime."

"Did they sell you out?" Martin asked.

"That's a lie."

Martin told him about looking for Slam and Slime at the club and getting abducted. Martin didn't mention Agent Tanaka. He decided to hold some cards for later use. "Somehow I woke up here."

"Doesn't mean my men turned. Maybe Nikos had his men follow you." Flavian snickered. "Who are you? A PI or something?"

"Nope. I restore classic and muscle cars."

"You a mechanic?"

"I mostly do paperwork in the office." Martin decided not to mention Dad either. Or any other member of his family.

Flavian laughed. "I asked for a muscle man, not a muscle car man."

"Sorry to disappoint you."

"Get some sleep."

The last thing Martin wanted was to sleep in this foul prison. He closed his eyes and prayed to God for mercy.

And a swift death if needed.

~

A small stream of light came through the slit of a window far above Martin's head, but it was enough to wake him up from his uncomfortable slumber on the concrete floor.

He took inventory of his surroundings, but there was nothing much to report. The floor was dusty and grimy. Cobwebs hung above him here and there, but he could not see any spiders. He hoped they were the friendly neighborhood kind. Garden variety spiders or harmless ones that he could tolerate.

Five or six feet away, Flavian slept on his back. His pants were ripped and caked with dried blood. One ankle was askew on one leg, and the other knee bent the wrong way. He must be in terrible pain.

But he seemed to be sleeping, albeit noisily.

How long had he been in here?

Was he really Corinne's ex? Ex what, exactly? Boyfriend? Fiancé? Husband?

Who was Nikos who had thrown them in here?

Martin tried to remember what had happened to him, but his recollections ended at the moment he passed out in the nightclub.

The last face he had seen was FBI Special

Agent Tanaka. Had she been abducted too? If so, where was she?

And whatever happened to Pilar the PI?

Were Corinne and Dahlia somewhere in this building too?

Flavian groaned, and then cried in his sleep.

Martin guessed the man might be in his forties. Early forties, maybe. Martin couldn't place his ethnicity, and he couldn't tell if Corinne's daughter looked like him.

Someone tell me what's going on and who everybody is!

Martin heard noises outside the door. Then the door opened and two bowls appeared on the floor just inside the door. Sticking out of each bowl was a plastic spoon.

The door slammed shut.

"Would you mind getting my bowl for me?" Flavian had woken up.

Martin nodded. Well, he didn't mind, so he should have shaken his head. Whatever.

He picked up the dirty melamine bowl, and wondered what that gook was. It looked like a cross between oatmeal and grits.

Martin handed the bowl to Flavian. "I'd ask what happened to you, but it's clear they beat you up."

"Broke my legs so I can't get out of here." Flavian dug into his breakfast.

"How long have you been in here?" Martin sat down up against another wall.

"I don't know, to be honest. I went to Key Largo after I found out what happened to Gail..." He pursed his lips, but Martin could see his chin tremble a bit in the morning light.

"What happened to her?" Martin asked quietly.

Flavian described the assault in the dark lane in some detail that Martin didn't think he needed to hear. He went on to talk about hiring someone to kill the rapist who had defiled his ex-girlfriend, and then stationing Slam and Slime to watch over Gail until now.

He was on his way home to Las Vegas when he was carjacked. Next thing he knew, he was in this prison.

"Carjacked? Cor—Dinah—Gail was also carjacked."

"If it works, why change the method?" Flavian pointed his plastic spoon at Martin. "You want to eat your breakfast? I don't mind having seconds."

Not knowing when he might be allowed to eat again, Martin declined the offer. He bowed his head and thanked God for the food. He wondered if this had been how Joseph felt after he had been thrown into prison in Egypt. The Bible story from Genesis was one of his favorites.

Then he prayed for Corinne, Dahlia, Pete, Angelina, the police, the FBI, Tanaka, Corinne, Dahlia, whatshisname over there, Dad, Tina and her husband, Corinne, Corinne, Corinne...

His prayer was all over the place.

When he opened his eyes, his food was still in the bowl. He forgot for a moment that there was not a chance Flavian could crawl his way to grab the bowl out of his hand.

"I thought you fell asleep," Flavian said.

"I was praying. Talking to God."

"Ah, God. If there's a God, why are we still in prison?" Flavian asked.

"I don't know."

Flavian tried to change position and winced.

"You need a doctor," Martin said.

"I need a priest. Last rites and whatever you call it." Flavian made hissing sounds through his gritted teeth.

"I wouldn't know about that." Martin ate up. It tasted like bits and pieces of soggy cardboard stirred into dirty water.

"Huh?"

"My church doesn't do last rites."

"What kind of church is that?"

"We believe that when we Christians die, we go straight to heaven to be with Jesus Christ, our Lord and Savior," Martin explained.

"Just like that?"

Martin nodded. "II Corinthians 5:8 says, 'We are confident, yes, well pleased rather to be absent from the body and to be present with the Lord.' My ticket to heaven has been bought and paid for by Jesus Christ. You believe?"

"Nah. Fairy tales."

"When you see God, it'll be too late, man."

"I'm my own god."

"Sure. And here you are." Martin put down the bowl. The plastic spoon clattered in it. It was so flimsy there was no way he could turn it into a weapon so they could stab their way out of here.

Maybe the next stop for him was really heaven.

Martin prayed that God would take care of his family and Corinne's family too if he didn't make it out of here.

He even said a prayer for Flavian's salvation.

CHAPTER TWENTY-FIVE

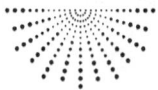

*I*f there was one thing that Flavian had taught Corinne, it was to use guile to get her way. Flavian had thought that she might become an able confidant to him in his business and activities. Little did he know that she would become an FBI informer, leave him, and take his only child with her.

Lying there on her prison bed, awake just before dawn, Corinne stared at the small slit of a window where morning light was crawling in across the ceiling.

She longed for freedom.

"Set us free, Lord Jesus." Her whispered prayer rose up to heaven. "I don't want to live in fear like this the rest of my life. I want to be free to take

Dahlia to school, to church, anywhere, without looking over my shoulders. Thank You, Lord, for the brief freedom in Key Largo. I pray that You'll give us more of it—of sunshine, a yard to play in, beaches to walk on..."

Corinne touched her belly. Someone else's baby was in there—

No, my baby.

"You're mine now, little one. I'm your mommy."

But neither Dahlia nor the unborn baby would have a father. Corinne shifted position on the bed, and a tear streamed down her eye.

Regardless of how many people Flavian had killed, Corinne would have to admit that he had been a good father to Dahlia the first two years of their daughter's life.

Someday, if she ever saw Flavian again...

No.

How quickly have I forgotten all the people Flavian had killed to get to those diamonds?

Now, Nikos might kill her and Dahlia just to get to Flavian—if he hadn't already. Unfortunately, whether Flavian was dead or alive, there was no way Nikos could get to half the diamonds.

Because I have given them to the FBI.

Corinne had no idea what time it was, but she knew that in the last three days, someone came to escort her to breakfast shortly after dawn. Nikos was either an early riser or he didn't sleep at night.

She prayed for strength at what she was about to do. Before she could finish praying, she heard footsteps outside the door. Boots on cement or whatever the hallway floor was made of.

No doubt they had come to take her to breakfast. This time she told herself to be brave enough to ask for a shower and clean clothes.

She heard the key turn on the other side of the door.

She prayed again.

She half-expected that Miss Executioner would come for her, but this wasn't her job. Usually a couple of guards would escort her out of here. They'd go up one flight of stairs, and walk down a wide hallway to an airy room overlooking the bay.

She didn't remember seeing any boat docks outside, but if she could take Dahlia outside, she could try to find a boat to get off the island. Or wait until one arrived.

But first, she had to get out of her cell.

She sat up on her bed. That way, she wouldn't arouse suspicions. Didn't want the guards to think she was too eager about a potential plan or something.

As soon as the guard opened the door, Corinne spoke. "Is there anywhere I can take a shower?"

The guard stared at her.

"I also need clean clothes since I've worn this for four days."

The guard said nothing, as if stunned by something.

"Please ask Nikos for me, will you?" Corinne realized then that if she had been in this position three years ago, she would have flashed a bare thigh or shoulder. Flavian's men would bow immediately, especially Slam and Slime, so easily bought.

Not any longer.

She was saved in Jesus Christ now, and her old life was dead to her, including everything she had to do in Las Vegas to survive.

Sometimes she wished she had never left Savannah.

Wished she had married Martin instead when he asked her to four years ago.

And bore his children inside a Christian marriage, instead of having two kids by different fathers and ending up as a single mother.

"Tell Nikos I'm not going to see him until I get a shower and some clean clothes."

Who in their right mind would choose to stay in a cell? It was no bargaining chip. And it was certainly not the type of guile that would make Flavian proud of her.

Asking for a shower was buying time. Corinne figured that if she could see more of the house—the building—then she might know the escape routes.

She regretted not asking Flavian more about the building. He had told her the bare minimum. She should have asked him about boats.

Half an hour later, she was escorted by none other than her maid-in-waiting, Miss Executioner.

"You take everything, don't you?" She snarled. "You take my man, my child, and now you take my clothes."

"Clothes? I only asked for a shower."

"Nikos said you need a change of clothes." Miss Executioner pushed her forward. "He wants you to shower in my bedroom, and then change into my clothes. He wants you to look like me."

"You're taller than I am." Corinne wasn't sure if that helped. Perhaps she could...

"Of course, I am. I'm also better than you. But Nikos has his eyes on you because you belong to Flavian."

"I belong to God," Corinne corrected her.

"Don't go there."

"You mean heaven? If I die now, I go to heaven because I trusted Jesus in my heart,"

Corinne said. "Do you know where you're going?"

"I'm going to get my man back."

"I mean after you die."

"I'm not going to die any time soon."

"You will when they come for me." Oops. Corinne shouldn't have said that.

"They who?"

Uh... "Flavian's people."

"Slam and Slime are dead, woman." Miss Executioner shoved her into the sparse bedroom, and led her to the bathroom. "Your clothes are on hangers."

"I don't get to choose?"

"Nikos has already chosen." Miss Executioner's voice cracked.

Suddenly Corinne wasn't afraid of her anymore because she had found Miss Executioner's weakness.

One word: Nikos.

Corinne hated to do it, but if she kept pushing the Nikos button, she might be able to disarm the woman when she was most vulnerable.

She took her time in the hot shower, shampooing her hair at least three times. The hot water never felt better.

She dried her hair with a towel, and put on the

too-big blouse. The stretch pants fitted her loosely. She rolled up the pant legs until they cleared her feet.

Miss Executioner was waiting for her outside the bathroom.

"Do you have a hair tie?" Corinne asked politely.

"No. Let's go." Miss Executioner turned slightly, and Corinne took the chance.

With a flying kick, she knocked Miss Executioner over. While the latter was regaining her balance and reaching for her gun, Corinne spotted the Taser around Miss Executioner's belt.

Corinne yanked it off the belt, and tested it on Miss Executioner, who writhed in pain.

Then Corinne took Miss Executioner's handgun and key card.

CHAPTER TWENTY-SIX

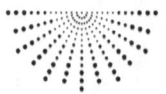

*M*artin stood up as soon he heard commotion and screams outside their cell.

Flavian laughed. "I think she did it. All those lessons finally paid off."

"Who?"

"Gail." Flavian tried to get up.

Martin shuffled toward him. "You can't walk with broken legs."

The door clicked and opened.

"Flav—" Corinne's eyes widened when she saw him. "Martin? What are you doing here?"

"Keeping Flavian company." Martin lifted Flavian. The man wasn't too heavy, just about as much as he could bench press at the gym.

Okay. Maybe just a tad more.

"You know who he is," Corinne said.

Before Martin could reply, he heard another voice coming from the hallway.

"Hurry up! Let's go!" Agent Tanaka stood at the door. She looked disheveled. Her hair was matted, and the clothes she had worn at the night-club that night were torn in various places, but she had handguns in her hands and a two more hanging off an oversized vest.

"Now!" Tanaka yelled again.

The four of them went up the stairs, with Flavian piggybacking on Martin and giving directions on which hallway would lead to the outside. He was in great pain as his broken legs dangled on both sides of Martin's waist.

Tanaka led the way, and Corinne brought up the rear, behind Martin who was carrying Flavian.

"I have to get Dahlia." Corinne pulled away.

"Corinne!" Martin stopped in his tracks.

"Corinne? Why did you call Gail that?" Flavian looked puzzled.

Everyone ignored him.

Tanaka walked past Martin and Flavian. She shoved a handgun into Martin's waist. "You two go ahead. Flavian knows the way out."

"Corinne." Martin was too stunned to say anything else but: "I don't want to lose you again."

"You never lost me. Go. I'll see you later." Corinne started sprinting, Tanaka at her heels.

Martin's heart warmed. He heard her words over and over in his mind.

You never lost me.

"What did she mean by that?" Flavian asked.

Martin couldn't reply. He wanted to cry. Flavian wasn't heavy, but his own heart was.

What if those were Corinne's last words to him?

He had to get Flavian out of the building and then he decided he'd return to help Corinne and Tanaka.

Then again, what could he do? It was apparent that Corinne knew how to use a weapon.

And that she was buddies with Tanaka.

Was Corinne an FBI informant?

Was that why she ended up in WITSEC?

The door opened to heavy rain. Martin's steps were slowed down by the part-sandy and part-muddy ground. He nearly slipped once or twice, with Flavian hanging on to his neck with his one good arm.

A sudden force pushed Flavian against Martin's head, throwing him off balance. He slipped and fell face first into the ground. Flavian slid off his back. They both groaned in agony.

In the thunder and lightning, Martin heard gunshots. And more groaning from Flavian.

"They're coming!" Martin got on his knees, but he had lost a shoe. He tried to reach for Flavian.

Flavian was not moving on the ground.

"Flavian?" Martin crawled toward the man.

Like thunder, a host of boots pounded around them, heading toward the house. Martin looked up but saw nothing until a flash of lightning gave him light.

Large words were emblazoned on the back of the vests of the crowd of armed people.

FBI.

Martin was so relieved he rolled back, flat on the muddy ground. He closed his eyes and let the heavy rain pelt his face.

He didn't stay long before someone knelt down beside him. "Can you walk?"

Martin nodded. Tried to get up. From the corner of his eye, he saw two FBI agents carry Flavian. He followed them. It was a long walk through a grove of trees that smelled like oranges, but they made it to a dock.

Two boats awaited them. From the markings, Martin guessed that one was a Coast Guard boat, and the other looked like a Marine Patrol boat from the Miami Beach Police Department.

All that told Martin they were off the coast of Florida somewhere, but not quite on international waters if the local police had jurisdiction.

Where are we, really?

The thunderstorm had passed, leaving what felt like a tropical shower.

A helicopter landed on the flat grassy plain next to the dock. Paramedics poured out and started treating Flavian. He was still not moving.

Martin's thought that Flavian wasn't that seriously injured when he carried him went out the door when he heard what the FBI agents said to the paramedics.

Gunshot wounds.

Martin quickly said a prayer for Flavian.

Another paramedic approached Martin. Suddenly all his muscles hurt from having to carry Flavian. He stretched out on the ground. Rain fell on his face and soaked through his clothes.

Everything else moved in slow motion around Martin. All he could think of now was Corinne. Was she alive?

You never lost me.

Did she really mean it?

The paramedics told him to get to a doctor

since he didn't have any broken bones or gunshot wounds. That meant Flavian had taken a bullet for him.

A bottled water appeared in front of him. It was Pilar Santiago with a smile on her face. "You're alive."

"You're alive too." Martin grinned.

"Someone had to call 911 and contact the FBI." Pilar sat down next to him. "Told you to stay in the van."

Martin ignored her chastisement. "What happened to you in the club? We waited a long time."

"I never left. I was in the back alley looking at two dead bodies." She was specific about saying *two*.

"Let me guess. Slap and Spit?"

Pilar shrugged. "Don't know their real names, but they're dead now."

"Turncoats can't be trusted by either side."

"We don't know what they are."

"Nor do we care." Martin drank half the water. "How did you know we were here? What is this place anyway? I don't even know where we are."

"You're on a private island off the coast of Florida. It's owned by a trust fund. Your captors rented it."

"Let me guess," Martin said. "Because it has prison cells in the basement?"

"Does it?" Pilar whistled. "Do they give tours?"

"Flavian wasn't our captor," Martin said.

"I know. It's his ex-business partner whom Agent Tanaka has been trying to take down for a couple of years."

"That still didn't explain how you found us." Martin finished off the bottled water.

"Tanaka injected herself with a tracker, but Nikos must have discovered it because the FBI tracked it to the bottom of the sea outside Miami Beach. That's why it took two more days to look for y'all. Kudos to the Coast Guard who helped the police."

Martin's eyebrows rose. "Did you say two days?"

"Yeah, happy Friday." Pilar suddenly stood up. "Here they come."

Martin watched a group of people emerge from the orange grove. On the other side of the grove of trees, smoke rose into the dark early afternoon sky.

An FBI agent carried Dahlia. Corinne and Tanaka came up behind them.

Martin was relieved to see Corinne.

You never lost me.

Corinne didn't look his way, though. She

screamed and made a beeline for the stretcher lifting Flavian into the chopper. She hunched over the injured man. When Dahlia was handed to her, the chopper lifted off in the rain.

Martin's heart sank to the bottom of the sea. Maybe the words she had spoken weren't meant for him at all. Maybe they were meant for Flavian.

You never lost me.

CHAPTER TWENTY-SEVEN

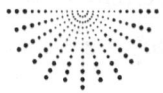

lavian was in surgery for hours, first to get the multiple bullets out of his back, and then to put his broken arm and legs back together. Corinne wondered about the pointlessness of the latter procedures because the surgeons had told her that he would never walk again, thanks to his destroyed spinal cord.

But first, he had to regain consciousness.

Pacing back and forth in the hospital playroom didn't do her any good, but she didn't want to leave Dahlia, not after what had happened yesterday.

Corinne's mind was numb. The entire episode felt surreal to her, as though she hadn't been there in person. It was a coping mechanism she had perfected over the last four years.

Her feet hurt and she sat down. Her ankles had started to swell as her pregnancy progressed. All this stress wasn't doing her a bit of good.

But she had to be strong for Dahlia.

Someday she might tell her daughter everything that happened in the first three years of her life. Yet, Corinne had been pushing the memories further and further back into her own forgetfulness to the point that she wondered if she'd remember them clearly when the time came.

Watching Dahlia color with chunky crayons, Corinne began to tear. She prayed that her daughter would be strong growing up, that her life would be easier than hers.

And that she would find God at an early age.

Corinne dared not close her eyes as she prayed for Flavian. She glanced at the clock on the wall, ticking away the pains of her life.

Here she sat alone with her daughter.

Well, not really alone. Outside the playroom, a Miami Dade police officer sat on a chair. Corinne didn't know whether to feel safer with him there or be alarmed that someone was still after her—according to Agent Tanaka, who had gone hunting for Oscar.

Corinne didn't believe she was in any danger, but Tanaka was sure that if Flavian didn't have the diamonds Nikos wanted, then someone else had them. Oscar?

Apparently the smuggled stash was bigger than either Corinne or Tanaka had thought. It had turned out there were more diamonds out there somewhere, beyond what Flavian had traded and what Corinne had handed over to the FBI.

Nikos was dead.

Corinne couldn't get the picture out of her mind. As soon as she and Tanaka had stormed the room where Nikos was playing house with Dahlia in the toy kitchen, the FBI agent fired two shots into the man's head. No questions asked.

Later, Tanaka would say that she thought Nikos had nefarious plans for the little girl, still in pajamas.

But Nikos had never touched Dahlia in the years he had visited Flavian and Corinne in their mansion outside Las Vegas. He wasn't a predator, as far as Corinne knew. He was only using Corinne and her daughter as leverage against Flavian.

Then again, both had ordered the killings of their enemies. They lived by the sword, and now they would die by the sword.

Flavian was still alive, though.

Corinne prayed again. *Let me speak with him one more time, Lord. Please.*

She heard footsteps and voices. She straightened up.

The surgeon she had spoken to earlier appeared at the door.

Corinne leapt up, and then found herself hobbling toward the doctor. "Is he all right?"

"Mr. Bailey is in a coma in ICU," the surgeon said.

"May I see him?"

"Soon."

"Will he live?" Corinne asked. It was more for the sake of her daughter. Their daughter. Flavian was still Dahlia's father, after all.

"We don't know. We lost him twice in the OR."

Corinne gasped. "Let me see him ASAP."

The surgeon nodded.

~

*W*as it possible to talk to a comatose person about Jesus Christ? Could he hear her speak and pray? Corinne didn't know.

But she was going to try, nonetheless.

Suited up with a mask and gloves, Corinne walked gingerly into the ICU. While she felt that it was an overkill, the nurses had told her that Flavian was in such bad shape that they didn't want him to catch more germs and get infections. He would be wheeled back into more surgery soon.

Corinne knew that the FBI wanted him alive because he was the little fish that could lead them to a bigger fish. That was, assuming Flavian would cooperate with the authorities, something he hated doing all his life, and which had led him to be as elusive as possible.

It was astounding to her that the FBI could not find any way to charge Flavian before. Granted, he had been on their radar only for four years.

Whoever they were after must be worse than Flavian.

Was it Oscar? Or was Oscar yet another little fish?

Flavian was all bruised and bandaged. He had an oxygen mask on his face, machines all around him.

Gently, Corinne squeezed Flavian's hand—on the arm that wasn't bandaged.

No response.

Corinne held his hand. "Flavian?"

No reply.

"Flavian, I have something important to tell you." Corinne gathered her thoughts. She leaned against his ear. "I know you can't speak right now, and you're not awake, but I hope you can hear me."

Flavian didn't move from his position.

"Jesus died for us, for all our sins." Corinne's voice started to crack. "He saved me. He can save you too. It's not too late."

No movement.

"Jesus carried our sins—all of them—at the cross over two thousand years ago. He knew what you would do, what I would do." Corinne began to weep softly. "Ask Him to forgive you of your sins. He is ready to redeem your soul right now. No matter what you have done in your entire life, He can still save your soul."

Corinne patted his arm. "God loves you, Flavian. He sent His only Son, Jesus Christ, to save you from your sins. Believe in Jesus now—"

Beeeep! Beeeeeep!

Corinne looked up. There was a long horizontal line on one of the monitors. She heard alarms outside the intensive care unit. Nurses rushed in.

"Ma'am, you have to leave now!" They ushered her away from Flavian.

Outside, Corinne watched in horror through the glass window as nurses and doctors surrounded Flavian, trying to revive him.

Again and again and again.

To no avail.

CHAPTER TWENTY-EIGHT

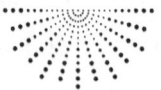

From Pilar, Martin found out that Flavian had passed away at the hospital. Martin wanted to be there for Corinne, but Agent Tanaka said she wasn't available. The only way Martin could see her was if Corinne herself asked for him.

He prayed that she would.

Her job done, Pilar had driven back to Key Largo to pack up her things and check out of her hotel. Before she left Florida for good, she wanted to have coffee with Martin.

Martin was in no mood for coffee, but he met her anyway at a beach restaurant near their hotel. He had returned to Key Largo with Pete and Angelina.

It was Saturday afternoon, hot as can be, and yet there were sunbathers on the beach, roasting their skin—and their children's skin.

Speaking of children, Martin wondered how Dahlia was doing. The poor child was now fatherless, although something else could be said about having a criminal for a father. A father was a father, regardless.

Thoughts of Dahlia led Martin back to Corinne.

And he lost his appetite for the soup in front of him.

Across their outdoor table, Pilar seemed to be studying him. "I talked to Tanaka. Corinne is grieving. Give her time."

"She said, 'You never lost me.' I thought she was talking to me, but now I wonder if she meant Flavian." Martin turned away from Pilar, embarrassed at having spoken his mind.

"Fog of battle." Pilar finished her salad. "The next time you see Corinne, ask her to clarify her statement."

"I wanted it to be me, but..."

"It must be awful to be in such a circumstance." Pilar asked the server for a refill of her lemon water.

"Have you ever been in love?" Martin asked, trying to take his own mind off Corinne.

"Well..." Pilar seemed to be thinking about the question. "Yes and no. Yes, when I was sure he was the one, but no, when he was clearly not the one."

"Are we talking about the same person here?" Martin chuckled.

"Yes, unfortunately."

"How long ago was it?"

"Six months ago."

"I'm sorry. Must have hurt."

"Worse than a gunshot wound, I can tell you."

"That bad?" Martin had no idea what that meant since he had never been shot before.

The last time they tried to shoot Martin, Flavian had taken the bullets in his spine, and lost his life the next day.

"I tell myself that God is sovereign," Martin said. "I couldn't leave Flavian behind. I had to carry him out. His legs were broken, you know? I couldn't leave him behind."

"You said that twice."

"I know, but I couldn't leave him behind." Martin blinked. "The only way to get him out of there was to put him on my back."

"He became a shield for you." Pilar leaned back in her chair. "Like you said, God is sovereign. When God protects you—or provides for you—in unexpected ways, don't question it. Accept that

God is sovereign over life on earth. It is His to give life and take away life."

"But Flavian might not be saved."

"I would caution you not to say *but*. That could mean that somewhere in your heart, you're judging what God allows."

"He allowed it. I agree with that."

"It might not have been His perfect will, but He allowed it for a reason that we may never know while we're on earth."

Martin nodded. He recalled witnessing to Flavian while they were in the cell together. God had allowed that too, hadn't He? Perhaps that was the last time Flavian ever heard the Gospel.

Then again, surely Corinne would have also witnessed to him.

Flavian had plenty of opportunities to get saved.

"Look," Pilar said. "I can't promise anything, but since Tanaka and I are sort of friends now, I will ask her again to let you have a few minutes with Corinne."

"Why can't they let me speak with her? She needs me now." Even as he said it, Martin wasn't sure if Corinne needed him. Of course, she needed God more. Besides, their island experience proved that Corinne could hold her own.

No, she doesn't need me.

On the other hand, I need her. I need her badly.

"I didn't want to let her go four years ago," Martin said. "She left without saying goodbye. Now she might leave again."

"Although if she does, you'll know that it's most likely for her own safety—and that of her child."

Martin nodded. They were in an open air restaurant, a public place of sorts, and he could not mention names. That much, he knew from Tanaka's debriefing.

In fact, Tanaka had given him strict rules about his time on the island. He couldn't talk about it to his sister or his parents. He couldn't talk about it to Pete or Angelina. Or Ming, for that matter.

The only person who knew a little bit of what he went through was Pilar, and she wasn't much help in the emotional support department.

Pilar's phone rang. She checked the message, and stood up. "I have to take this call in my car."

"I'll take the bill," Martin said as Pilar left him.

He waved to the server, refused dessert, and paid for everything in cash.

Suddenly paranoid, Martin wasn't about to use his credit card which might put him...

What am I talking about?

He felt a heaviness in his heart.

As hot as it might be out there in the sun, Martin felt that he had to walk off his stress. He put on his sunglasses, and walked across the hot sand.

He was ankle-deep in the Atlantic Ocean, walking without a thought in his head, when he realized someone was walking next to him.

"Keep looking ahead." The whisper was soft.

Corinne.

"Isn't it unsafe for you to be here?" Martin whispered back, but he didn't look at her.

"Yes and no. Don't look now, but I'm wearing a wig."

"I recognized your voice."

"I know."

"I have so many questions."

"I don't have time to answer them." Corinne sighed. "I can't be at Wanda's funeral. Or in public as myself."

"That's tough. I don't know what's going on but I need to know if we can see each other again."

"Maybe never. All our lives are in danger."

Martin stopped walking. "That serious?"

"Keep walking," Corinne said.

"Where are you going?"

"I don't know."

"Who will be a father to your children?" Martin asked.

"God the Father takes care of widows and single mothers."

"Let me help."

"I don't need help. I can fend for myself. I've been fending for myself since I was a teenager."

"I'm sorry." Martin choked up. "I didn't mean that way. I don't want to let you go, and I'm trying to find a reason for us to be together."

"Pray that this situation is only temporary. You know they're looking for the third person. Until then, they're putting Dahlia and me in a safe house." Corinne drew a deep breath. "I can't even attend Wanda's funeral."

"Too public." Martin nodded. Flavian and Nikos were both dead, but Oscar was still at large. Somewhere in their lunch conversation, Pilar had said that the INTERPOL was after Oscar. Drug and diamond smuggling, plus human trafficking.

"Until they find him, my daughter and I have to disappear again," Corinne said quietly.

"I want to go with you," Martin said suddenly.

Corinne was speechless.

"Let me go with you."

"No, Martin." It was a firm response. "Go home to Savannah. Your family's probably worried about you by now. Get on with your life."

"I found you again."

"You never lost me, Martin."

Martin stopped. Tears pooled in his eyes. Man tears, he told himself. Man tears. "I thought you meant that for..."

"For my ex?" Corinne held Martin's hand. "You never lost me. You never left my mind. He never had me."

"Wow. So it was meant for me, after all."

"Yes. If you must know, I had to sell my body to survive, but that doesn't mean I wasn't concerned about his salvation."

Martin flinched. Oh, how he wished he had somehow prevented Corinne from leaving Savannah four years ago. Then she wouldn't have—

No. In fact, because he loved her, he had to let her go. She had to make her own choices. If she wanted to be with Martin, she had to decide to do so. He couldn't make her or force her to do anything. It wouldn't be love.

"I'm a survivor, Martin. I'm not a victim," Corinne stated.

"I'm glad."

"It was the darkest time of my life," Corinne explained. "God used it to bring me here, where I got saved—the brightest time of my life. Key Largo will always be a special place to me because this is where I met Jesus."

"God worked it all out for your good," Martin said.

"Yes, He did. And for Dahlia too. I wouldn't raise her anywhere outside the church, to be honest. That has been my sanctuary."

"Your sanctuary is Jesus." Martin didn't mean to correct her, but there it was. "A person, not a place."

"Of course. Jesus is my sanctuary. I have a lot to learn yet as a Christian."

"We're all learning." Martin swallowed. "I'm learning right now that I'm dying at the thought that I can't be with you any more."

"That's why I came. I knew you needed closure."

"Closure? No." Martin stopped walking. He faced Corinne and realized not only was she wearing a wig, she was also wearing makeup that made her look like someone else. The oversized tee-shirt with a vest on top covered her baby bump. "Are you really Corinne?"

Corinne barely nodded.

"I loved you once and I love you still. Marry me, Corinne." He was on his knees.

"Get up get up get up." Corinne sighed. "I should never have come."

"No, I'm glad you did." Martin brushed off the

sand stuck on his knee caps. "Sorry, that was a knee-jerk reaction—literally."

Corinne chuckled. Then her voice sounded more serious than before. "Both of us are Christians, right?"

"Yes."

"Our lives belong to God. We are in Christ, our life and hope. We don't have to worry about each other. Remember that."

Martin nodded.

"If you must know, I never stopped loving you. Often, I wondered what it would have been like if we had married four years ago. If I hadn't run away. If I hadn't..."

Martin stopped her with a kiss on her lips, soft and warm—but it could be the Key Largo sunshine.

Now her lips tasted like salt...

Martin opened his eyes. Tears were flowing in rivulets down Corinne's cheeks. "Shhhh."

Corinne wrapped her arms around his neck and drew his head toward her.

"Finish the kiss," she whispered through her sobs.

They walked a little further before Corinne spoke again. "God will keep us safe in the shadow of His wings."

"Amen."

"Look it up. I think it's mentioned in both Psalm 57:1 and Psalm 17:18."

"Right now?" Martin didn't want to let go of her hand.

"Uh-huh. God's Word cleanses our soul."

Reluctantly, Martin let go of Corinne's hand. He dug for his phone and started swiping. Looked for his Bible app. "What were the verses again?"

No answer.

He lifted his head.

He was standing alone.

Around him, families and other beachgoers were either packing up or already walking toward the stairs leading to their vehicles or hotels, driven away by the hot sun.

He didn't see Corinne anywhere.

She was gone.

CHAPTER TWENTY-NINE

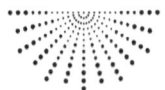

Four long months had passed since Martin returned to Savannah, back to work. Dad questioned how his Shelby was messed up, and all Martin could say was he had been in a fender bender outside Key Largo. Everything else had to be kept a secret.

"Did you see Corinne?" Everyone asked, from Dad to his wife to Tina to her husband. "Where is she now? Has she ghosted you again?"

"Stop asking me about her." And that was the end of it.

He didn't want to think about Key Largo, about the love lost, love found, and love lost again.

Yet he knew now, more than ever, that he loved Corinne. No matter what she had gone through, the blood of Christ had cleansed her sins from her —past, present, and future.

He would have to surrender her to God. There was no other way.

He couldn't call up the FBI hotline and ask for Agent Tanaka.

The only hotline he had was to God's ears. He prayed in the Name of Jesus Christ that God would protect Corinne, Dahlia, and the new baby.

He prayed that God would bless them and keep them safe and draw them close to His heart.

He prayed that God would fill Corinne's heart with eternal love, endless peace, and everlasting joy —all found in Jesus Christ.

Still, Martin wondered how she was doing. She was probably six months along now. Three more months and the baby would be born.

Martin decided that he would sell his 1966 Shelby to Dad, and put the money aside for Corinne and her children. If she didn't need it now, she could keep it for their college funding in the future. He had no idea how he was going to let her know or give the money to her, but maybe Pete and Angelina could help later on.

He wondered what else he could do. He would give up his career if it meant he could see Corinne again. He would give up the whole world for her.

Then again, he had no idea what was happening with Corinne now. Was she still in hiding? In a safe house somewhere? In WITSEC? Helping Agent Tanaka?

Or perhaps, had she married and moved on?

Maybe she could if she didn't love him as much. However, Martin knew he couldn't move on.

He would be a bachelor for the rest of his life.

~

*T*hanksgiving at Mendenhall Retreat was quiet as there weren't many small children around. In fact, Dahlia was only one of a few children there at their hiding place because they were in danger.

Larina Brannigan, the director of the facility, kept the kids occupied during the week with Bible studies and classes at their grade level. Dahlia was the only three-year-old, but in four months, she was reading books meant for four-year-olds. Needless to say, Corinne was delighted at the progress and forever grateful to Larina.

Every little bit helped. Corinne did some work for the retreat center, helping Larina and her office manager, Phoebe O'Tierney, with some office work. After all, Corinne had been trained as an office manager herself in her previous line of work—back in Savannah when she worked for Martin's sister at her pottery studio.

By November, Larina increased Corinne's pay as she filled in for Phoebe, who took two months off to take her children to see her husband's family in Ireland.

Phoebe had better come home by the end of December because Corinne wouldn't be able to cover for her any later than that. Baby Liam was due at the end of January.

Corinne didn't mind working there, but the uncertainty of her future was another reason not to get attached to the place and atmosphere.

The four months of hiding away in this place, without being able to visit the nearby mountain town, was making her feel claustrophobic. She didn't know how much longer she could take it.

Still, it kept her alive.

Here, nobody would come for her. According to FBI Special Agent Tanaka, she and Dahlia would be safest here.

When pressed, Tanaka divulged that there was a mole inside the FBI that had compromised their informants' whereabouts, including their transfers to the WITSEC program. Without authority, Tanaka took Corinne off the grid and brought her and Dahlia here, a remote secret retreat on the top of the Great Smoky Mountains at the border of Tennessee and North Carolina.

Dahlia had been confused at first, but her nightmares about her dying father subsided in November when snow fell, blanketing the log cabins and walkways.

When Corinne wasn't working, they stayed in their cabin. Sometimes they cooked fresh vegetables from the retreat garden. Sometimes they ate at the lodge.

Like tonight.

It was Thanksgiving Eve, but Corinne planned to stay indoors all day on Thanksgiving Day, so tonight was their turkey night.

Sitting at a corner table and talking very little to strangers who had nothing to say to her, Corinne ate quietly and thought about her life up until now.

Mostly, her thoughts turned to Martin.

He had proposed to her on the beach that day back in July. She didn't give him an answer. She thought he was probably emotional and not thinking straight.

They had just met again after four years apart, so how could he be so sure he wanted to marry her.

Unfortunately, it was the second time in four

years he had proposed to her, and both times, Corinne had disappointed him.

She could never...

Well, *never* was such a severe word.

Sitting beside her, Dahlia was falling asleep. It was only about seven o'clock in the evening, but Corinne had trained her daughter to go to sleep by eight. That way, Mommy had time to herself for a couple of hours to read the Bible and take it easy before she went to bed.

Alone.

As soon as Corinne finished eating, she asked for a takeout bag. A server cleared her plates, so she didn't have to leave Dahlia by herself with a bunch of strangers at the dinner table.

However, when Corinne tried to carry Dahlia, she felt that the girl was pushing too hard against her womb. The seven-month-old baby kicked his big sister.

Corinne had to let Dahlia down, but the little girl didn't want to walk. She was starting to whine.

"No whining," Corinne said sternly.

Through the windows, she could see that it was snowing harder now. How could she walk uphill with a griping child? The last thing she needed was to fall in the last trimester of her pregnancy.

She prayed for wisdom.

When she stopped at the door to take a deep breath, she heard someone call her.

The Mendenhall Retreat co-director came her way. Larina always smiled when she saw Corinne and Dahlia. On the other hand, her husband, Joseph, the other director, often wore a scowl, as if everything was deadly serious.

And perhaps it was.

Mendenhall Retreat, Corinne found out, wasn't like any other mountain resort. Its guests ran the gamut from people in the military and government to private security companies. They came here to recharge and rest before they launched back into their work and career. Some others came to hide and wait until the danger was over.

Corinne learned never to ask questions, and to assume that many might be using nicknames or false identities.

Larina Brannigan wasn't her real name. And no, Corinne wasn't allowed to ask about her life. All she needed to know was that Larina led a women's Bible study at the retreat every Monday, Wednesday, and Friday.

Every Sunday, the Mendenhall Chapel held services, and so did the Misty Mountain Chapel in the nearby town. While trusted employees were allowed to go to town, Corinne wasn't. Not until danger passed.

To keep her and Dahlia safe, she had to trust Larina completely. That's what Agent Tanaka had told her.

"Happy Thanksgiving to you and Joseph." Corinne smiled, getting the attention of the octogenarian. "Are your kids coming to town?"

"Oh, they can never come here, as you know."

"Ah, yes. I forgot."

"No worries." Larina gazed at the sleeping Dahlia. "If you ever need a babysitter..."

"Thank you. I will let you know." Corinne put the pink winter coat on Dahlia. She slept through it all. Corinne would have to carry her out.

"If you stay here long enough," Larina replied.

Corinne nodded. "It should be over soon."

"I hope so, but if you have to stay through your baby's birth, I'm fine with it. We have a discreet OB/GYN on my rolodex, and the bill will be taken care of."

"Delivery too?" Corinne teared up. God had indeed provided for her in so many ways she hadn't realized.

"And postpartum. Don't worry about anything."

Corinne nodded.

Neither broached the subject, but as soon as the FBI caught Oscar, Corinne would be free.

Even if it made no sense for Oscar to come after her, there was no way to prove to him that she had no idea where any more diamonds were. That information went with Flavian to the grave.

Outside, the snow fell harder, and beyond the porch and parts of the parking lot, it was pitch black. Her cabin was way up there on the side of the hill.

Uh-oh.

Larina stepped in front of Corinne and closed the door. "I think I have a spare room upstairs. Maybe you can go back to your cabin in the morning."

"That's a great idea. How much would it cost?" Corinne asked.

"I told you. Everything is included."

"I heard you, but I thought that's only for the cabin and food. Oh, and everything else."

"It's a deal." Larina gave Corinne the room number and key card. "You better take her up before your arms break. There are toiletries in the drawers near the sink. Stay there until morning or sleep in until lunch or later. Whatever you prefer."

"Wow. This is the life." Corinne laughed. "Eat and sleep all day."

While she was taking it easy here, she wondered what Agent Tanaka and her team were doing. Life must be hard for law enforcement people, continually chasing criminals. Corinne couldn't even begin to understand.

All she knew was that God had protected her and her daughter all the way.

As she walked toward the elevator taking her to her room for the night, she said a quiet prayer for Tanaka. For safety and success.

Then she prayed for Martin. That God's perfect will would be done in his life, regardless of whether His perfect will included Corinne or not.

Lord, I surrender Martin to You.

CHAPTER THIRTY

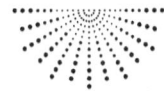

wo weeks after Liam was born and two days after Valentine's Day, FBI Special Agent Tanaka showed up at Mendenhall Retreat, bearing gifts and accompanied by another agent, Stella Evans.

Corinne was alone in her cabin that afternoon. She had just nursed Liam and put him down for a nap—hopefully a long one—and was about to take a nap herself when the doorbell rang. At first she thought it might be Larina bringing Dahlia back from preschool.

It wasn't.

Tanaka had been here once before, but that had been seven months before.

"Please tell me you have good news for me."

Corinne invited them to her small living room in the cabin.

The living room was small and it was comprised of a sofa, a small armchair, and a coffee table. Beyond that was a small dining table placed in the middle of the kitchen.

The one bedroom was upstairs, where two single beds were flanked by a new bassinet for Baby Liam.

Corinne kept her voice down. "My baby is sleeping."

Tanaka and Evans nodded.

"Would you like some tea or coffee?" Corinne asked.

"Water is fine for me." Tanaka sat down on the small couch. "I drank too much coffee this morning."

"Whatever you have is fine." Evans walked past Tanaka and sat on the armchair.

"I can't drink any caffeine since I'm nursing Liam, but if you'd like tea, I'll boil some hot water." Corinne studied Evans.

"That's perfect." Evans swiped her phone. Then looked at Tanaka as if to ask her to take the lead.

"Gail—I mean Dinah—I mean Corinne." Tanaka laughed. She kicked off her shoes and stretched out on the sofa. "I'm so tired. Why can't Oscar just give himself up?"

"Wouldn't that be easy for all of us?" Evans chuckled.

Corinne put a pot of water on the stove and covered it. She carried a kitchen chair with her to the living room and sat down on it. "How can I help you?"

"I've already told you more than I should," Tanaka said. "But you had to know so that you'd be careful wherever we put you, right?"

"I appreciate that." Corinne realized then that she was still wearing the sweatshirt and sweatpants she had on the night before. In fact, she hadn't showered. It seemed that these days, her life revolved around her new baby. There was no time for self care.

There should be, she told herself.

"Evans is here to ask you some more questions so that our investigation can proceed and get to a satisfactory conclusion."

Corinne turned her attention to Evans. "Well, I know I won't be safe until Oscar is caught. However, Oscar has many enemies. He's a patient man and will hide for as long as he can. I don't want to be living here for years."

Evans nodded. "I know. We're doing our best, ma'am."

"From the bits and pieces you've told me, and from my own knowledge of how Flavian, Nikos, and Oscar operated, I'm gathering that the operation is ongoing, and I'm stuck here for the foreseeable future."

Evans and Tanaka stared at each other and then at Corinne.

"Many of our informants are in danger," Tanaka admitted.

"You're here to tell me that I can't go home." Corinne would love to go back to Key Largo. To see Pete and Angelina and everyone else at church again. To send Dahlia to school. To get a decent job somewhere. To live a normal life.

"Like I said, we're doing our best," Evans repeated herself. "I can't tell you much more than that."

"So why are you here?" Corinne tried not to lose her patience. But any time now, her baby could wake up, and then their conversation would be over. "If you need my help, I have already told Agent Tanaka before that I can't remember too much about the years I was with Flavian. I was abused and I blocked most of the days from my memory banks. However, if you ask me pertinent questions, maybe they will trigger a memory or more. You know what I mean?"

Tanaka sat up. "I told you, Stella. I would like to trust her, or else more informants will die."

"Die?" Corinne nearly fell off her chair.

Tanaka nodded. "We're having a crisis. That's why we had to go outside the FBI to get help. That's why you're here at this hideout instead of at a documented safe house."

"Have you talked to Esperanza Diaz-Mendenhall?" Corinne asked. The owner of Mendenhall Retreat was also the leader of the Mendenhall Security team that did undercover work and special operations all over the world.

"Actually, we have a meeting with her after this." Tanaka pointed to the kitchen where the pot of water was boiling.

Corinne didn't even hear it. It wasn't a whistling kettle, after all.

As she made loose leaf tea for Evans, she heard Tanaka saying she'd like a cup too, if it wasn't too late. "No, not too late."

Corinne wished she could have a cup of hot tea too. The weather outside was still cool this February, but unseasonably warmer than past years, she heard. No snow this month so far.

She carried the two cups on a tray, with a bottle

of honey, just in case anyone asked. She didn't have sugar in the house, so she didn't bother asking them if they wanted sugar.

"Sorry I have no sugar, but I do have slices of frozen lemons," Corinne said.

"This is fine. Thank you."

As they sipped their hot tea, Tanaka began to broach the subject.

Since the days Corinne had known her as Stephanie, her non-cousin in Hawaii, Tanaka had been forthcoming with her—as much as she could. To gain Corinne's trust, the agent had told her all the horror stories of how bad Flavian really was behind Corinne's back.

Corinne had known much of it, and wasn't surprised by any of it.

Now it was about Oscar, a little-known business associate of Flavian's.

"I'm assuming you don't have Oscar because whatever information I gave you didn't help," Corinne said.

"No, no. It helped," Tanaka said.

"We just need more," Evans added.

"He's elusive." Corinne knew that much. It was in the interest of her daughter and son that Oscar was caught as soon as possible.

Yes, Dahlia and Liam.

Corinne closed her eyes to whisper a prayer to God for her children. She didn't care what happened to herself, but she knew that she would do everything for her children, even if she had to sacrifice her own life.

Yes, she would go that far.

The log cabin was quiet. Outside, no birds chirped. No vehicles roared by. Any time now, Corinne would hear footsteps on the porch, accompanied by Dahlia's giggles or laughter as Larina walked her home from preschool.

Home? Hardly. This was still their mountain safe house, all because danger had not passed by.

Corinne recalled the two verses she had left with Martin the last time they kissed on the beach in Key Largo. Was it in July? Seven months ago now.

She wondered if Martin had looked up the verses in his Bible app. Whether he did or not, it was between him and God. It wouldn't change her memory of him.

Yet somewhere in her heart, she hoped he had read the verses, especially Psalm 57:1, which she had committed to memory.

Be merciful to me, O God,
be merciful to me!

For my soul trusts in You;
And in the shadow of Your
wings I will make my
refuge,
Until these calamities have
passed by.

Regardless of whether she had memorized many verses yet, the most important thing in her life was her salvation in Christ, making her a new creature in Christ, as her Bible told her in II Corinthians 5:17.

Therefore, if anyone is in Christ, he is a new
creation; old things have passed away; behold, all
things have become new.

Corinne had memorized that verse in the first year of her salvation. Her journey as a Christian had continued in weekly Bible studies at church, where she studied more verses to infuse into her new life. She had been studying the Bible ever since, with God renewing her mind day by day, and filling her heart with the love of Christ.

She thanked God for the assurance again and again. "New in Christ. Blessed thought indeed."

"What blessed thought?" Tanaka asked.

"II Corinthians 5:17." Corinne opened her eyes.

"Ah yes. 'Old things have passed away' and 'all things have become new.' I like that verse," Evans said.

"Are you a Christian?" Corinne asked.

Evans nodded.

"Well, whatever floats your boat," Tanaka said.

"My boat was sinking fast until Jesus fished me out of the deep waters." Corinne looked at Tanaka and Evans intently. "Now God has brought you here to keep my family safe."

"Great." Tanaka smiled. "Which leads me to Oscar."

Oscar.

"He's not in Cuba?" Corinne asked.

"No. He fled Cuba. We don't know where he is."

"If you think Flavian and Nikos were bad..." Corinne didn't want to fear again.

"Glad you mentioned Flavian and Nikos. Since they're dead, we can't interrogate them," Tanaka said. "However, we figured that if we knew more about those two, we might be able to extrapolate where Oscar might be hiding."

"Once we find him, rest assured we will put him away for a very long time," Evans added. "If you must know, we need him to connect the dots to a terrorist at large."

Corinne knew whom she was referring to. "It's Molyneux, isn't it? A few years ago, I overhead Flavian say that Oscar works for her."

Evans's eyebrows rose.

"I told you she can help us," Tanaka said.

"I try to forget many things," Corinne explained. "Because I value my life."

"We'll protect you."

Corinne studied Tanaka. The veteran agent meant what she said, but she couldn't protect anyone more than God.

Keep me as the apple of
    Your eye;
Hide me under the shadow
    of Your wings,
From the wicked who
    oppress me,
From my deadly enemies
    who surround me.

In Psalm 17:8-9, the psalmist prayed that God would hide him under the shadow of His wings, even as his wicked and deadly enemies surrounded him.

That was the other verse Corinne had shared with Martin. Did he still remember even now, seven months removed?

Martin? Why did Martin's name pop up?

Maybe if this entire mess was over, Corinne could be free to live again. Then she could visit Martin, if he still wanted to see her. There were so many things she wanted to tell him.

Including giving him the answer to his question.

Until then, she had to trust God to protect her.

Hide me in the shadow of Your wings, Lord Jesus. Don't let me be afraid.

"If you don't help us, more informants will die," Tanaka said.

Corinne shifted in her chair. "You haven't caught your mole."

Neither Tanaka nor Evans replied.

That told Corinne a lot.

She drew a deep breath. "Ask me anything."

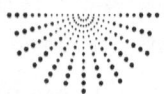

CHAPTER THIRTY-ONE

One year to the week since Martin had been in Key Largo, he arrived again to visit Pete and Angelina at their invitation. Apparently, those two had become an item, gotten married, and now lived in Angelina's houseboat.

When Martin pulled up at the parking lot next to the waterway, Pete was outside washing his truck. He stared at Martin's rental car and shook his head.

"You didn't drive your Shelby here." Pete dunked a rag into a bucket of water.

"Nice to see you too." Martin locked the car, and pushed his sunglasses to the top of his head as he made his way to Pete.

Pete wiped his soapy palms on his tee-shirt and

shook Martin's hand. "Glad you could come for lunch."

"Want me to help?" Martin looked at the bucket. He was wearing shorts and a pair of dock shoes, but if they got wet, he had a change of clothes in the trunk.

"No need. I'm just going to spray some water all over it and be done." Pete picked up a water hose. "I don't want your clothes to get wet. Just talk to me while I do this."

Pete made a quick job of rinsing off his car. "I'll let the sun dry it all afternoon before I wax it."

"I'll help."

"If you want. But I can't pay you."

"I take double desserts."

"Have all the desserts you want!" Pete led him inside the houseboat.

As Martin stepped onto the wooden deck, he recalled talking with Corinne here at this very spot a year before. It was a sunny Sunday after church, and several church members had gathered here for lunch. Angelina had cooked spaghetti, and Corinne brought her daughter.

Martin wondered where Corinne was these days, whether she had moved on. There was still the matter of the college fund he had started for her children. How would he be able to tell her about it?

And yes, he wanted to tell her in person. Not to brag, but to see her face, to let her know he really cared, even if they weren't meant to be together.

One year later, and Martin couldn't move on.

There was no way he could move on.

Corinne would always be in his heart, and memories of her would be everywhere in Key Largo.

He felt like he was grieving someone. Truly, it felt like Corinne had died, and he would never see her again.

"Whoa! Have you gained weight?" Angelina shrieked.

"Nice to see you too." Martin laughed. "Well, yes, I have gained about twenty pounds, but I blame Thanksgiving pies and Christmas cookies."

"And here you asked for double desserts." Pete laughed from inside the houseboat.

Martin followed Angelina through the door, half-wishing that Corinne was there.

She wasn't.

The small living space looked more cluttered now, with the armchairs and sofas pushed closer together to one another. And across the rug from a big screen television was a giant leather recliner.

"Have a seat!" Pete plopped himself down on the recliner, as if saying, "Anywhere but this chair."

"Turn the TV off," Angelina told him.

"I haven't turned it on," Pete replied.

"You were going to!"

Martin laughed. "What are you watching?"

"Nothing since she sent me out there to wash my truck." Pete threw his arms up.

"You had the news on, and you were getting upset by the minute," Angelina said from the open kitchen. "I didn't want your blood pressure to go up."

Martin walked past Pete toward Angelina. "May I help?"

"Yes, you may." Angelina sounded pleased that someone offered to help. "You can help me set the table."

"Tell me where the plates and silverware are." Martin washed his hands at the sink.

"I'm glad you washed your hands...unlike some people." Angelina laughed.

"I heard that!" Pete said from the other side of the peninsula.

All Martin could see was his head over the recliner. He had turned on the television—in spite of Angelina's protests—but he switched over to YouTube.

"Turn it down," Angelina said.

Pete dutifully did so. "I'm going to see what news I missed."

Martin could see the television from where he was standing by the small dining table. He set three place settings. Then he filled three goblets of cold water.

"...is now behind bars as he awaits trial..."

Martin ignored it. Same old news every day. Crimes everywhere. *So what's new?*

"Did you hear that, Martin?" Pete asked.

"What?"

"It's Flavian's associate."

Martin nearly dropped the last goblet of water on his way to the dining table.

Flavian.

Corinne's ex-boyfriend.

For Flavian's eternal sake, Martin hoped that he had somehow accepted Jesus Christ as his personal Lord and Savior before he passed away. Even if he couldn't speak, but had made the profession of faith in his heart, it would be enough. From his heartfelt plea to God's ears.

Otherwise it would be a very dark eternity for him.

Once again, Martin wondered how Corinne was doing.

Well, I'll never know.

Carefully, he placed the last goblet on the dining table and went to the living room. "What's happening?"

Pete pointed to the screen with his remote. "They caught Oscar with no last name in Cuba. He was an associate of Flavian and Nikos. It was all coming out now that they were a trio of diamond smugglers. Oscar's job was to convert the diamonds into weapons for terrorists."

"No kidding." Martin had to sit down. "Wow."

Corinne had been in way more trouble than he had thought.

"I wonder what Corinne went through those years she had been with his ex," Pete said.

"We won't talk about the past any more." Angelina's voice cracked. "All we can do is pray for Corinne and her babies. Her newborn must be at least four months old by now."

"I do miss them," Pete said.

"Me too," Angelina chimed in.

And I miss her most of all.

Spaghetti lunch was served, and Pete asked Martin to say grace before their meal. Martin made a short work of it, but he ended it with a prayer for Corinne.

"Lord, I know You're watching over Corinne and her two children, but I want to keep praying that You would not let any harm come to them. If those criminals and diamond smugglers are gone, I pray that she will be free again. Above all, I only want Your perfect will to be done in her life. In Jesus' Name I pray. Amen."

Everyone else said *amen*.

Their lunch conversation turned to their present-day life, and Martin realized that the two of them were living in poverty.

"What do you mean you don't have health insurance?" Martin asked.

"We have Medicare," Angelina said. "But Pete here put his life savings and the profits from the sale of his house into an investment fund that went under."

"Oh, no." Martin felt sorry for the man. "You lost money."

"All of it." Pete barely nodded. "I thought my nephew was... Well, I shouldn't have trusted him."

"So now he needs to get a job," Angelina added. "You know anyone who could use a retired mechanic who can't see straight without trifocals?"

Martin didn't know whether to laugh or cry.

"Don't worry about me," Pete said. "Angelina talks too much. It's not as bad as she's making it."

Martin ate his spaghetti quietly. Angelina kept

giving him more. By the time he had three helpings, he was too full to eat any dessert.

"I made coconut macaroons," Angelina said.

"Well, I'll have one." Martin laughed.

When Angelina passed the tray to her, Martin took four or five. They looked too delicious to pass up.

As he chewed, he turned his attention to Pete. "If you wear your trifocals, you can still see, right?"

"Sure." Pete straightened up. "I can see fine. Angelina just worries about me."

"You can't even afford to get your eyes checked and get new glasses." His wife patted his arm.

"Why are you saying all these things in front of our guest?" Pete chided her. "It's not polite."

"I was hoping he'd offer you a job at his car place." Angelina looked at Martin.

Martin hadn't thought about that, but if Pete qualified, there was no reason not to hire him. If he knew enough about classic cars to be useful, he could be helpful to Dad.

"In Savannah?" Pete asked his wife. "I don't know."

"If you go to our website and search for the Careers tab, you can find the job openings," Martin said. "Dad handles that part of the company. He's the personnel director. I mostly deal with paper-work and taxes and such."

Pete looked embarrassed.

"You'll have to move to Savannah though," Martin said. "There are fewer hurricanes there."

"We'd have to sell this boat," Pete said. "Or rent it out."

Angelina nodded. "Maybe I'll get a job there too."

"At MacMuscles?" Pete's eyebrows rose.

"No, silly." Angelina laughed. "In Savannah. Or on Tybee Island. We'll still be by the Atlantic Ocean."

Martin remembered her skillset. She was good with details. Suddenly he remembered something he heard at church on Sunday while he was chatting with his friend, Hunter Jacobs. His aunt ran a campground, and was looking for someone to help her in the office a few days a week.

"I can't promise anything, but I heard about a job at a campground office. It's part-time, but it could be a start," Martin said.

"Where?"

"Tybee Island. It's not on the beach, but near it."

"Pete, go apply to MacMuscles and see if they hire you and I'll apply to this place." Angelina turned to Martin. "Campground? They rent cabins and such?"

"I think they have yurts."

"Yurts?" Pete helped Angelina put away their plates. "If we sell this houseboat, we could buy an RV and live on the campground. Save some money."

"If God wants us to do this, we'll do it," Angelina said. "I almost forgot to say we need to pray about this first, but then again, we have been praying for God to deliver us from our financial difficulties."

"Yep. And in the middle of it, we got a call from you, saying you'd like to come down here for a few days, for old time's sake." Pete nodded to Martin. "I'm glad you could have lunch with us. I know it's hard for you since it's been a long year, but I hope you found our friendship comforting to you."

"Thank you for inviting me."

"And that we haven't unloaded our personal issues on you." He glanced over to Angelina, loading the dishwasher.

"If you don't ask, you don't get," Angelina quipped.

"That's for sure." Martin carried two goblets back to the kitchen. "We do have a turnover of mechanics. So apply for the job and see. I will mention this to Dad, but I won't sway him one way or another."

"I don't expect you to."

"He already knows that you helped Corinne when she was here in Key Largo. Dad appreciates compassionate people."

Pete nodded. "I still can't get used to her being called Corinne."

"She will always be Dinah to me." Angelina chuckled. "But what's in a name? God knows our real names."

"Indeed." Martin asked Angelina if she wanted him to pour the rest of the iced water from the goblets on a plant or something.

"Your mother taught you that?" Angelina asked as she told him about her container plants on the deck outside the living room.

"My stepmother, actually. She doesn't waste."

"That's good."

Martin went outside and poured the ice out onto a rosemary bush and a tomato plant. They looked healthy and well-watered. The tomato plant hadn't flowered yet.

Under the containers, the small deck floated on top of the waterway. Beyond the waterway, the water flowed toward the ocean, which Martin couldn't see from here. A couple of boats chugged by, and Martin waved to them.

Key Largo was a nice place to visit, but could he live here?

Even as he asked himself that question, he knew he couldn't without Corinne.

Not without her.

Then again, he knew he had to let her go.

CHAPTER THIRTY-TWO

*I*t didn't take much time for Pete and Angelina to pack up, sell their house-boat, buy a recreational vehicle, and move to Tybee Island. They parked their RV at Jacobs Landing Glamping Camping, and Angelina found a job at the manager's office working for Delilah Jacobs, who ran the campground.

Martin knew about the campground because some of the Jacobs family members attended River-side Chapel. Delilah's nephew, Hunter, was once in the same Sunday school class as Martin before Hunter married and switched to a class for young marrieds. Apparently, Hunter had been the one to make his aunt drop the apostrophe in the name of the campsite if Delilah refused to call it Jacobs's Landing.

Regardless of Delilah's grammatical issues, she had shown only kindness to Pete and Angelina. Delilah discounted their extended stay on account of their age, and invited them to the Super Seniors Bible study group at church.

During the week, Pete turned out to be a hard worker at MacMuscles Classic Car Restoration and knew so much about engines that Martin's dad had taken a liking to the man. It helped that they had both been in the service, and they were about the same age. Both were grandfathers with grandkids out of town.

By September, Pete and Angelina had settled into their new life in Savannah and Tybee Island, with a little help from Martin. Forever grateful, they often invited Martin over for dinner on random nights. Martin wasn't always available, but he tried his best to eat with them once a month.

This time, they had postponed dinner twice. Angelina twisted her ankle walking on the uneven grounds at the campground, tripping over a tree root. They had to cancel dinner so that Angelina could rest.

Martin only agreed to the raincheck because Pete promised to grill hamburgers. Frankly, Martin was getting tired of spaghetti every time Angelina cooked. How many ways could she cook spaghetti?

Tasked to bring a dessert, Martin picked up a pecan pie from Piper's Place in downtown Savannah on his way to Tybee Island. The pie wasn't very big, but it was enough for three people to have seconds.

Martin was late by a few minutes because he had a business meeting with Dad about the feasibility of opening a small branch of MacMuscles in Miami. Dad pointed out that Martin was grasping at straws if his thought of Miami and that part of the region had anything to do with an ex-girlfriend.

Corinne had been gone for over a year. In fact, thirteen months, two weeks, and a few days.

No one had heard from her or of her. In fact, Agent Tanaka had also vanished. When Martin tried to contact her at the FBI regional office in Savannah, he was told that no such agent worked in the FBI.

Basically, just go away.

Perhaps Tanaka had been fired. Perhaps she had gone incognito. Perhaps she was even dead.

What about Corinne?

Martin parked the SUV in front of Pete's RV, but didn't get out of the car.

"Lord, please take care of Corinne and her children. I know You have, You do, and You will. Just let me—teach me—to trust You and not be so worried out of my mind." Martin leaned back against the headrest. "I mean, is she even alive?"

He willed himself to get out of the car. After locking it, he dragged himself to the door of the RV. Before he reached it, Pete appeared around the back of the RV. He was wearing a brightly colored apron.

"Glad you could make it." Pete waved with his spatula.

"Ah, I forgot the pecan pie in the car." Martin went back to get it.

"See you around back where the grill is."

"Okay." The smell of hamburgers wafted over and around the RV into Martin's nostrils, and suddenly he was famished. After getting the pecan pie out of the backseat and locking his vehicle door, he quickly followed the smell of food.

"Hello, Martin!" Angelina was limping around a folded table under a canvas canopy, putting condiments in the center of the table. There were no chairs around the table, but there were four camp chairs under a string of lights.

Four chairs.

Martin freaked out a little, wondering if the fourth chair was for...Corinne?

His hopes were dashed when an old ginger cat leapt up into the chair and settled down, going to sleep.

"A cat chair." Martin handed the pecan pie to Angelina.

"Yep." Pete flipped the burgers. "He came wandering into our RV one day when the door was open and that was it. He hasn't left."

"A stray cat?"

"Delilah said he usually comes and goes but rarely stays."

Angelina stroked the cat's head. "This time he chose us."

"How old is he?"

"At least ten or fourteen. I don't know." Pete chuckled. "Angelina named him."

"He came to us when there was a heavy downpour, and it looked like the campground was going to be flooded," Angelina explained. "So we called him Sunshine."

"Better than Umbrella," Martin said.

"Umber for short. Hmm." Pete turned to Angelina. "Hand me a platter, will you, my dear?"

Soon they were sitting down on their camp chairs. Even though Pete asked Martin to say a blessing over their dinner, Angelina didn't say amen when Pete was done.

"And Lord, please watch over Corinne and her two children, Dahlia and whatever his name is," Angelina prayed. "In the mighty, powerful, all-sufficient Name of Jesus Christ. Amen."

"Amen," everyone else echoed.

"How do you know the baby is a boy?" Pete asked.

"I'm guessing. I think she wanted a boy." Angelina smiled. "Martin, if you ever have children, would you want boys or girls?"

"Anyone God provides." Martin realized too late that he had answered quickly.

"Oh, you've thought about it." Angelina gave him a sly smile.

"Not really." He backtracked. "My sister, Tina, has three kids. When I visit her in Atlanta, I spend a lot of time with her kids. I'm their favorite uncle— their only maternal uncle."

"That's good practice for you."

"I don't know." Martin felt he was saying it honestly. "I might be a bachelor the rest of my life."

"I don't know about that." Angelina tipped her head up. "I think you're the marrying kind."

"What on earth does that even mean?" Pete laughed.

The rest of the evening, they made small talk all the way thorough dinner and dessert, surrounded by citronella candles holding back mosquitoes. It was September now, but the mosquitoes were still out.

Martin noticed that Angelina was quieter than usual. Perhaps her twisted ankle was still giving her problems. Perhaps she was on medication. Perhaps she was simply tired from all that work at Delilah's office.

"Thank you for the dinner." Martin wiped his lips. "That was an excellent hamburger."

"Welcome," Pete and Angelina said in unison. "Want more?"

"No, no. I'm full—except for maybe a piece of pie."

"Good pie," Angelina said. "So they make all sorts of pies at Piper's Place?"

"Yes. And lots of cupcakes too." Martin thought that maybe for Christmas, he could give them a gift card to Piper's Place.

After Pete sent Angelina inside to rest her ankle, he and Martin made short work of cleaning up the place. They let the grill cool down, and Pete said he'd clean it up in the morning.

"Is everything okay?" Martin asked as they took out a bag of trash to the large dumpster down the lane.

"You mean me or Angelina or us both?" Pete asked.

"Both, I guess."

"I'm doing fine." Pete tossed the bag of trash into the bin. "Angelina is probably a little homesick."

Did that mean Martin was going to lose Pete? He had only started work in late July. Two months and no vacation collected.

"Are you going home at Christmas?" MacMuscles gave everyone a week off then for family time.

"I think she wants to go home now."

"Oh."

"She has this idea that she shouldn't have sold the houseboat. She thinks Dinah is going to show up one day."

Corinne.

Angelina still called her Dinah.

Martin wished Pete hadn't brought up Corinne. Now he felt lovesick, like his heart should be in Key Largo, waiting for Corinne to show up. "I do miss the place."

"And people." Pete picked up his cat and sat down on his camp chair.

Martin sat down next to him. "It's been about fourteen months. Didn't we watch the news back in July about them catching that Oscar dude?"

"Maybe he was only a little fish and they needed him as bait to catch a bigger shark. Then it would take a while longer for the whole thing to be done."

How long? "Could be. We never know."

"If Angelina and I move back to Key Largo, will you think less of us?" Pete swatted a fly from his face. "I mean, I barely worked at MacMuscles for two months."

"Sometimes you have to leave a place to find out you want to stay after all."

"That's deep." Pete nodded. "We're praying about it, if you must know. If it's okay with you, we'd like to be home in Key Largo for good at Christmas."

"That's a good break. We get a week, as you know."

"I appreciate your creating a new position for me."

"Dad really likes you. You're a valuable part of our company." Martin meant it.

"Thank you, sir."

Christmas would be in three months, and then more goodbyes. Martin wasn't sure if he could handle it. Even though Pete and Angelina were not blood family to Corinne, they were the closest people Martin knew who actually spent time with Corinne.

"May I be frank with you?" Martin asked.

"Sure."

"If your heart is not in it, there's no point waiting another three months before you leave."

"We need the income to hold us over. Our retirement pensions aren't enough to live without working."

"Gotcha. Then work as long as you want. We just require two weeks of notice," Martin said. "All I ask is that when I do visit you in Key Largo, we could have lunch sometime."

"Of course. You're family now."

Family?

Why then did Martin feel so alone?

CHAPTER THIRTY-THREE

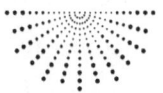

The 1967 L88 Corvette was lime green, shiny, and sleek. The engine needed a bit of work. When the MacMuscles finished fixing it and repainting it red, Martin could see himself behind the four-hundred-plus horsepower, cruising down the highway from Savannah to Key West.

The resale price tag was out of this world, but Dad didn't flinch. He eased into the driver's seat, apparently visualizing himself taking it out for a test drive.

The owner had passed away, left it to his wife, who then also passed away. Eventually, the car ended up with their granddaughter, who didn't want a two-seater convertible. She'd rather have an SUV and a nice big house instead.

"What do you think?" Dad asked.

There was Dad, sitting in a Corvette in the large garage, surrounded by at least eight other classic and muscle cars he had purchased at one point or another, including the Shelby that Martin had sold to him.

How many cars does Dad have time to drive?

"The price, Dad." It was all Martin could think to say.

"Life is short. I could sell a few of those cars over there." Dad waved.

"Because you want a lime green Corvette." Martin knew that red was Dad's favorite color, but it was only paint.

"I would be lying if I say I don't want it, but you know it's because I can repaint it red. How about we split this fifty-fifty?"

Martin hadn't told Dad about the educational fund he had set up for Corinne's children. Dad would question the wisdom of giving away money to someone else's kids when their mother had no intention of marrying Martin.

Well, Martin couldn't be sure it had been a resounding no. Corinne hadn't given him a definitive answer before she vanished from the beach right before his very eyes. How did she do it?

How did she blend into the crowd and disappear from his life?

The sun must've been in Martin's eyes that Saturday afternoon because for the life of him, he could not spot her anywhere. Perhaps she had been trained to blend into the crowd.

One year and three months later, Corinne's face was beginning to fade from Martin's memory. How many times had he wished he had taken a photograph of her when they were still in Key Largo? When he took out his phone to search for the verses from Psalm that she'd shared with him, he could have taken a picture of her.

Too late now.

When he asked Pete and Angelina for a photograph, they were just as surprised as Martin to find that most, if not all, of the photographs of Corinne at church events were either blurry, partially obscured, or too far away.

In essence, Corinne had purposely stayed away from center stage, from the spotlight.

Martin felt sorry for her, having to hide like that. If he had known that she was in WITSEC, he might have left her alone, considering she wouldn't be in the program had her life not been in danger.

However, pity wasn't why he had decided to save money for her children. It was...

Love?

To date, Martin had put in the equivalent of two muscle cars and one classic car into the fund. He had put away a few hundred dollars more each month.

"You want it?" Dad asked. "How about we sit in it for a while?"

"Knowing the engine needs work and we can't take it outside for a spin?"

Dad motioned for him to get in. "We'll take a selfie."

"That, I can afford." Martin laughed.

As he opened the passenger side door, he heard someone call his name. It echoed in the big space.

Martin...Martin...Martin...

Martin turned to see who needed him, and there was Pete, walking through the garage entrance and carrying a child.

Martin blinked.

The girl looked familiar.

Martin held on to the car door for support.

A stroller emerged in the sunshine, and behind the stroller...

Was Corinne Anderson.

In real life.

Her hair was longer now, and tied up in a pony tail.

Martin's eyes stung.

His knees wobbled. He leaned against the Corvette for support.

Lord Jesus, give me strength.

"Who's that?" Dad got out of the car.

When Martin and Corinne broke up six years before, it was only shortly after Dad had returned to his life. Dad probably didn't remember how Corinne looked.

"Someone we know?" Dad asked.

"The love of my life whom I couldn't have," Martin blurted.

"Corinne." Dad closed the car door. "Isn't that good news? If she's here, out in the open, it means she's out of WITSEC."

Yeah, Dad and Damaris knew about Corinne. Tina had told them as much as she knew. That way, she said they could be supportive of Martin.

He didn't need support. He needed...

Corinne.

And there she was, within reach. Martin wanted to sprint toward her, but his feet felt like they were cemented to the garage floor.

He swallowed.

Blinked again.

Lord, help me not to make a fool of myself.

"Hello! Who do we have here?" Dad said loudly as he approached Pete.

It was just as well that Dad made the first greeting because thirty-three-year-old Martin felt like an awkward teenager on his first date.

Corinne smiled to him. It was a warm and worry-free smile, as if the storms of her life were over.

Martin recalled the verse that Corinne had left with him on the beach that long-ago Saturday.

> *Be merciful to me, O God,*
> *be merciful to me!*
> *For my soul trusts in You;*
> *And in the shadow of Your*
> *wings I will make my*
> *refuge,*
> *Until these calamities have*
> *passed by.*

He had committed Psalm 57:1 to memory for her sake.

The fact that she was standing there testified that her calamities were over. God had indeed protected all of them for Himself.

Slowly, Martin made his way to the small group.

Not my will be done, Lord. Only Yours. That's all I ask. Help me to let her go if that's best for us.

"Corinne." Martin could barely speak.

Somewhere in the background, he heard Pete introducing Dad to Dahlia. "Tell Mr. MacFarland your name."

"Dahlia." She said softly, almost in a whisper, and quickly buried her face in Pete's shoulder.

"Hello, Dahlia," Dad said. "How old are you?"

Dahlia lifted four fingers.

"Four years old! My granddaughter is four too."

And on and on.

Martin's eyes were on Corinne.

"Hi, Martin," she said. "How are you?"

Dying inside. "Well. And you?"

"We survived."

"Praise the Lord. Been praying for you."

"I know." She smiled.

"You do?"

"Angelina told me."

"You've been to see her?" Martin wondered when she came into town.

"Stayed in their RV last night," Corinne said.

"Pete didn't say a thing."

"It was all last-minute. Agent Tanaka dropped me off in Key Largo, and I went to see Pastor Butler right away. We stayed at his house for a few days.

He told me that Pete and Angelina got married, moved up here."

"So you called Angelina."

"She still kept her old number." Her hands were on the stroller handlebar.

"I drove the kids up last night, and we slept all morning."

"I'm sure Pete and Angelina were happy."

"I came to see you, Martin."

Martin felt dizzy. "Say that again?"

And she did.

Martin wanted to give her a hug, but the stroller stood between them. Corinne walked around the stroller, and lifted the edge of a baby blanket. A cap covered the baby's head. The baby was still sleeping.

"Very cute. Boy or girl?" Martin asked.

"Boy. Liam. I named him after my father, whom they tell me is in heaven now," Corinne said quietly.

Martin wondered what it felt like for Corinne not to know her own parents. Even though Mom had died while Martin was in high school, at least he had some memories of her. Dad had left them years before, but returned when Martin and his sister were adults.

Corinne never knew her biological parents.

"Liam is eight months old now," Corinne added.

"Already?" Wow. Martin reached for her hand. "You look great."

"For a single mother with two kids?"

"I mean... I don't know what I meant."

"Cupcakes!" Dahlia suddenly said. "Mommy, please?"

Corinne glanced at Martin and then at her daughter.

Martin nearly laughed when he found both Pete and Dad looking like they were pleading for Corinne to say yes to cupcakes.

"Just one, okay?" Corinne lifted a finger.

Martin noticed that the bracelet was gone. In its place was a watch. He didn't know what that meant, and he didn't ask.

"Why don't we grandpas take the kids for a few minutes while you two catch up?" Dad said.

Thank you, Dad.

Corinne looked reluctant to let go of the stroller.

"We're just going around the corner," Pete said. "I'll text you as soon as Liam wakes up."

"Right away?"

"Instantly."

"Okay."

Pete put Dahlia down. "Can you hold Grandpa MacMuscles's hand?"

Dahlia shook her head.

"I'll push the stroller," Dad said. "You hold her hand."

And off they went.

CHAPTER THIRTY-FOUR

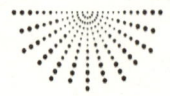

Martin and Corinne were alone in the cavernous garage.

"What is this place?" Corinne looked around. "Look at all those cars."

She was good at breaking the ice.

"These are my dad's cars," Martin said. "Want a mini tour?"

Corinne pointed. "That's your Shelby."

"It belongs to Dad now."

Corinne looked squarely at Martin. "You shouldn't have."

Martin sighed. "Angelina told you."

"I would've found out eventually. They're not your kids. Save money for your own kids."

"They're *your* kids. They matter to you."

"I don't need your help, Martin." She sniffled. "Because of me, you were in danger on the island."

Martin reached for her shoulder. She didn't brush his hand away.

"We're survivors, remember?" He reminded her. "Not victims."

"You remembered our conversation on the beach." She stepped away, walking toward the sunlight.

"Liam is fine," Martin said. "Pete said he'd text you."

She stopped. "Sorry I had to leave Key Largo abruptly. I couldn't tell anyone anything, not even you."

"I still don't know how you did it. You disappeared."

"The sun was in your eyes."

"More than that."

Corinne shrugged. "I followed a family leaving the beach. Long lost aunt or something. They didn't care. We were going up the same stairs anyway."

"So that's how you got away. I couldn't find you." Martin took the opportunity to ask more questions. "Where did you go? Where have you been for fifteen months?"

"They put us in a safe house. I was sworn to

secrecy regarding the location. No phone calls. No internet."

It was enough for Martin. "What did you do the entire time?"

"It was hard at first but I helped in their preschool."

"There were other families there?"

"I can't say more. I don't want to put other people in danger. One thing I can tell you is that I was surprised at how much I enjoyed teaching those little kids."

"I sense a new career path?"

Corinne nodded. "They gave me some reward money so I'm going to graduate school and get a teaching degree."

Martin didn't ask who they were. "Where?"

"Miami."

Miami. So far away.

"I have to get my GRE first, and then I'll apply for admission," Corinne continued. "Maybe for the fall semester."

"August?"

"Yeah. That will give me time to move to Miami and get settled in."

Martin didn't want to ask who was going to take care of her kids while she was in school. Corinne was independent enough to figure that out. She had to do what was needed to work and support her children.

"If you must know, Angelina has offered to watch the kids for me when I'm in class," Corinne said. "But it won't be until next year."

"I guess you heard that they're homesick for Key Largo."

"Thank you for finding them work."

"Only Pete. Angelina works elsewhere."

"I know, but Angelina said you put in a good word for her at Delilah's Landing."

"Jacobs Landing with no apostrophe."

Corinne giggled.

"Grad school, huh?" Martin tried to wrap his mind around it.

A long time ago, Corinne was an office manager. Then she became an FBI informant. And now she was going to be a school teacher.

So much had changed.

"What about you? What are you doing these days?" Corinne asked.

"Dad and I still run this place. We're still fixing old cars. I'm still in the office doing all the paperwork." Martin realized that little had changed in his career in the last several years. "I work at home some days so that I can look out the window and see the beach and ocean and think of you."

There. He said it.

"You mean they pay you to daydream?" Corinne laughed.

"I'm not daydreaming anymore. You're here. You're really here." Martin held her hand. Just one hand, in case he came on too strongly and she pulled away.

"And you were there for me," Corinne said. "Remember when you first showed up in Key Largo?"

Martin nodded.

"Looking back, I'm glad you went there to look for me."

"I had to know." Martin continued to hold her hand. "I often wonder if I could've gotten an answer from you that day on the beach."

Corinne's eyes brightened. That told Martin that she knew what he was referring to.

"It might have seemed abrupt and sudden, but I meant it," Martin said. "Under different circumstances—if you didn't have to disappear—would you have answered me?"

"I would have said yes."

Martin sensed no hesitation at all. It warmed his heart.

"Would you have said yes now?" Martin was on his knees.

Corinne gasped.

"This is not a knee-jerk reaction. Picture us on a beach." Martin's voice was soft and low. "Corinne Anderson, you're the one woman I've ever truly loved. Will you marry me?"

"Martin MacFarland, you never gave up. You're also the only man I ever loved. I never stopped loving you, even when I was far away from you." Tears streamed down her face. "Yes, I'll marry you."

Still on his knees, Martin held both of Corinne's hands. "I'm sorry I don't have a ring with me. I'll re-propose when I do, but we can pick our rings together if you like. I want you to like them and wear them the rest of your life."

Corinne pulled him to his feet.

"One more thing." Martin gently wrapped his arms around Corinne, as though she was the most fragile, the most precious person in the whole wide world.

"What is it?"

"Do you mind if Dahlia and Liam have my last name?"

"MacFarland's a long last name."

"So is Anderson."

"Well, maybe Anderson-MacFarland?"

"That's even worse." Martin chuckled. "That's a mouthful."

"And so is this." Corinne lifted her lips toward his.

Their kiss was warm and full of memories—of past grief, old sufferings, forgotten heartaches...

The good, the bad, the ugly had all been filtered out by the God of mercy and grace, the Holy God who picked up the shattered pieces of their lives and made all things new.

Of course, right in the middle of their reunion, Corinne's phone buzzed.

Corinne checked her text. "Liam's awake."

"Let's go," Martin said. "I want to meet my new son."

And he meant it.

CHAPTER THIRTY-FIVE

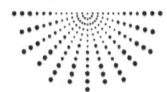

*E*ven though Corinne felt that their May wedding date was a long way off when she and Martin scheduled it, seven months raced by with major events happening one after another.

On the same day that Martin proposed to her back in October, he took Corinne to his stepmother's favorite jeweler in town, where they both picked her engagement ring and their wedding bands.

Engraved inside their wedding bands were the words "all things have become new" from II Corinthians 5:17.

When Corinne went home to Key Largo, Angelina went with her. She had quit her job at Delilah Jacobs's office. Pete stayed behind in

Savannah to work at MacMuscles for another two months until the Christmas break.

With Angelina now working as a full-time nanny to Dahlia and Liam, Corinne was able to start applying to graduate school, which she began to do after Christmas. While she was on a campus tour at the university, she discovered that the education department had jobs available. Since graduate school didn't start until August, Corinne decided to apply for one of the desk jobs at the office of admissions.

And she got the job.

Martin was surprised she applied for the job at all. It was true that she didn't need the money, considering the FBI had rewarded her three times for helping them to catch Flavian, Nikos, and Oscar —although she wasn't sure what kind of a *catch* dead people could be. Oscar wasn't dead yet, but if he stopped cooperating with the FBI and INTER-POL, they would turn him over to the FSB. That was the last thing he wanted.

By the time May came around, Corinne had spent the least amount of time preparing for her wedding. Not only was Angelina her nanny, she had decided to be her wedding planner as well, doing almost all the hard work of organizing and pretty much getting everything done.

"As long as we don't have a spaghetti rehearsal dinner," Martin warned.

It was truly one of the first few times when Corinne disagreed with Martin, while trying to take Angelina's side. At the end, she conceded that they better eat something else at the rehearsal dinner.

Speaking of Martin, Corinne was proud of him. Ready to get out from under his dad's shadow, he had worked hard to buy a fledgling auto shop in Miami and turn it into MacMuscles Miami, a small subsidiary of MacMuscles Classic Car Restoration of Savannah, Georgia.

By February, Pete was back working for Martin again, but this time they were both in Miami. Pete regretted selling his 1959 Volkswagen bus along with his house a while back before he married Angelina, but Corinne and Martin reminded him that it would be too stressful for his heart to look back and regret his decisions.

"Just turn the past, present, and future over to God," Martin said.

"We should put that in our wedding vows," Corinne added.

With Martin's help, Pete found another Volkswagen bus to restore. The kind man that he was, Martin let Pete keep his bus in their auto shop at no cost. The only condition was that Pete couldn't work on his own personal pet projects during work hours.

One month before their wedding day, Corinne and Martin found a house they liked. It had four bedrooms plus a home office and a fenced-in yard. The house was well maintained. The only thing they had to do was repaint the walls and replace the refrigerator and stove.

While Corinne especially liked how big each bedroom was, Martin was all over the large back-yard, looking for a place to put his new charcoal grill that his dad bought for him. How hard could it be to find a spot for his grill?

"It's a lot of yard for you to mow," Corinne pointed to the trees in the distance. "All the way over there."

"I'll get a riding mower." Martin smiled. "When Liam gets older, he can mow the lawn."

"He's only fifteen months old."

"Kids grow up fast."

"Yeah, they do. He's weaned already."

Martin wrapped his arm around her shoulders as they looked out at their future new yard. "Maybe we could have our wedding here."

"Hmm. Now that's an idea." Corinne held his

hand. "We aren't inviting too many guests. They can all fit in the backyard."

Martin kissed Corinne's forehead. "If we have more kids, they'll have a lot of backyard to play in."

"First things first, Mr. MacFarland. Let's get ready for our wedding."

After the closing, they had the house repainted, some appliances replaced, and the interior decorated in a southern beach-cottage style.

Corinne moved in with Dahlia and Liam first, while Martin stayed in Pete's small spare room a few miles away. Corinne wished that Pete and Angelina lived closer to them, but they didn't qualify for a house in this neighborhood.

Until Martin promoted Pete to General Manager of MacMuscles Miami.

For not discriminating against Pete's age, Martin found new respect in his fiancée's eyes.

Corinne also found out a few more things about Martin she hadn't known before, and that led to their decisions about a church for their family.

At the end of the day, they discovered that they both wanted to serve God in a local ministry of some sort. They would continue to pray about it and see where God led them. Pastor Butler had advised them to find a new church somewhere close to their home in Miami. It would make no sense for them to drive to Key Largo every weekend. It would be better for them to plug into a local church so that they could serve the greater Miami community.

The fact that Corinne and Martin had agreed on that and many other things about their new life together made her grateful to God.

Corinne knew that life would not always be filled with happy moments like these, but when blessings came, she reminded herself to trust the sovereignty of God over it all.

> *And he said:*
> *"Naked I came from my*
>   *mother's womb,*
> *And naked shall I return*
>   *there.*
> *The Lord gave, and the Lord*
>   *has taken away;*
> *Blessed be the name of the*
>   *Lord."*
> *In all this Job did not sin*
>   *nor charge God with*
>   *wrong.*

With the verse from Job 1:21-22 hidden in her heart, Corinne stepped forward onto the freshly mowed grass one glorious Saturday morning in the month of May. A perpetual smile on her face belied the fact that she was genuinely so nervous inside that she hadn't slept much the night before. She had been afraid that she wouldn't hear her alarm clock and then be late to the hairdresser.

Thank God that Angelina was staying overnight at the house, and she woke her up just in time to leave. Martin's stepmother, Damaris, had flown in from Savannah the week before to stay with them and help around with Dahlia and Liam as Angelina flitted here and there, preparing for her wedding.

A few hours after her hair and makeup were done, here she was.

The string quartet that Angelina found on the internet played a melodious medley of hymns. Budget-conscious to the bone, the wedding planner hadn't splurged at all. Her expense reports impressed Martin and Corinne to no end. They decided to give her a pay raise for her nanny duties.

Holding on to Pete's arm, Corinne prayed that God would let her own dad know that Pete wasn't trying to take his place. If her father had been alive, he would have walked her down the aisle.

All the guests rose to their feet, smiling to her as Corinne made her way toward Martin, who looked even more nervous than she was. His father was his best man, and he looked delighted.

Pastor Butler also smiled. He was holding the same worn Bible that he had used to counsel Martin and Corinne for several months before the wedding.

Corinne dipped her head and realized that she had been walking on haphazardly scattered flower petals on the grass. Those must have been thrown by her flower girl, Dahlia. Corinne decided she'd have to watch the video later to see it.

She also told herself to read the guest book to see who came to their wedding. She was afraid to look to her left and right. She felt that if she saw the faces of her friends and church family who stood by her through the rough times in her life, she would burst into tears and ruin her eyeshadow.

She spotted Damaris with her new grandson, the ring bearer. Corinne's breath caught when she saw Liam make a face in Damaris's arm. He was dressed in a pull-on stretchable baby tuxedo, but the moment he saw Mommy's face, he lifted his arms.

Uh-oh.

Damaris cooed and rocked him, pointing elsewhere. For a moment, his attention was distracted.

When Corinne reached the arch decorated

with orchids and hibiscus and other tropical flowers of many colors, she realized that Martin's eyes were filled with tears.

Don't make me cry.

After Pete gave Corinne away, she stepped up to the podium, smiling to her friend Ruby Tanaka. She had burned out after Oscar had been captured, and left the bureau shortly afterwards. Today, she was no longer FBI Special Agent Tanaka, who can kill with a single blow. She was only Ruby, Corinne's reluctant maid-of-honor.

There was no one else Corinne would rather have to stand with her at her wedding. Even while Tanaka had been undercover as Stephanie in Hawaii, she had looked out for Corinne all the way. When things got out of hand, it was Tanaka who rescued Corinne from the bad place, and found a safe house for her. She had put her life on the line many times to protect Corinne.

Somewhere along the way, the other agent had witnessed to Tanaka, and soon after Oscar was captured, she had accepted Jesus Christ as her Lord and Savior. In fact, Pastor Butler had baptized her in the Atlantic Ocean only a couple of months before.

In spite of the six-month-long preparation, the wedding ceremony itself went pretty quickly. Their vows were short and sweet and focused on God. Corinne was glad it didn't take too long because she thought Liam was about to burst into a wail when Damaris carried him to hand over their wedding rings.

Whose idea was it to make a fifteen-month-old baby the ringbearer?

Then Corinne reminded herself that their wedding theme was *thankfulness*. A near-disaster was an opportunity to be thankful.

The wedding favors that everyone would take from the reception to come included the verse from I Corinthians 1:4.

I thank my God always concerning you for the grace of God which was given to you by Christ Jesus...

"I now pronounce you man and wife," Pastor Butler said. "You may kiss the bride."

And Martin did. Long and sweet, with such an unabashed display of public affection, as if they wouldn't kiss again the rest of their lives.

The string quartet stirred up again, and the newlyweds strolled down the aisle, hand in hand, to the cheers and applause of the guests.

Corinne smiled to Martin's sister, Tina, and her

family. She spotted Ming and Sabine in the crowd. And she nodded to all her friends from Beach Town Church.

Then she turned her attention to Martin, who was beaming from ear to ear.

She loved this man. So down-to-earth and genuinely more caring than she had given him credit for all these years. Not only had he given up much for her and her children, he was totally fine with wherever they wanted to spend their honeymoon.

Corinne had to make him decide where to go so that he wouldn't blame her for it later on. And would anyone believe it if all he wanted to do was sit in a cottage looking at the ocean in Key West?

Well, that was what they were going to do all week on their honeymoon.

Their bags had been packed the night before and loaded into the tiny trunk of Martin's dad's new Corvette—once lime green, now painted red—for the three-hour drive to Key West, where they had rented an oceanfront beach house, complete with a personal chef so that they didn't have to cook.

Corinne looked forward to praying with Martin, reading the Bible together as a couple, walking along the beach whenever they wanted, and taking it easy without worrying about lurking dangers.

But first, the wedding reception.

After they stepped into their house, Angelina closed the door behind them to give them time to change in private. After that they were due to go back outside to a reception in a giant tent.

"How are you doing, Mrs. MacFarland?" Martin asked as they walked down the hallway to their master bedroom.

"It's surreal." Corinne thought her hands shook. She held her hands together.

"Are you nervous about our new life together?"

"I think I am."

"Me too." Martin wrapped his hands around hers. "Let's trust God to lead us forward."

Corinne nodded.

Their foreheads met and they closed their eyes.

"Heavenly Father," Martin began to pray, as if it was the most natural thing for them to do. "We give to You our new life together as husband and wife. Thank You for Your peace that passes all understanding. Thank You for bringing Corinne into my life."

He squeezed Corinne's hands. "We both want to be in Your perfect will now and for the rest of our lives. I pray that we would be godly to each other and to our children, and that we would handle all matters biblically, that our lives would be pleasing to You in everything that we think, say and do. Lord Jesus, may You be glorified now and forevermore."

"In the name of Jesus, we pray. Amen." Corinne closed the prayer for them.

"Now let's go change quickly before our wedding guests get any idea that we're busy doing something else that we're not doing right now."

Corinne chuckled, and laughed when Martin scooped her up and carried her all the way to their wedding chamber.

∾

DEAR READER:

Thank you for reading *Look for Me*, book 4 in my Vacation Sweethearts collection of Christian travel romances. While *Look for Me* is about second chances in Key Largo, Florida, the next novel, *Pray for Me*, takes us from the Bahamas all the way to Georgia, USA, to the Atlanta area where Midtown Chapel is located. Why would islander Augustus Moss want to spend his summer vacation in a land-locked city?

Pray for Me (Vacation Sweethearts Book 5):
JanThompson.com/pray

TINA MACFARLAND IS IN SMILE FOR ME:

In *Look for Me*, we meet several characters that have appeared in past books. For example, Martin's older sister, Tina, is the main character in *Smile for Me*, the first novel in the Vacation Sweethearts series. When Tina goes back to the Bahamas to teach in a summer art camp, she has to confront her nemesis, Byron Moss. Has their relationship changed two years later in this opposites-attract international romance?

Smile for Me (Vacation Sweethearts Book 1):
JanThompson.com/smile

MING WEI IS IN TELL YOU SOON:

Private Investigator Ming Wei, a church friend of Martin's, has his own story as well. We find him all over there in the Savannah Sweethearts coastal city and beach romance series, where all these Sweethearts book collections begin. In the *Tell You Soon* romance with suspense, Ming meets his future wife, Sabine Hu.

Tell You Soon (Savannah Sweethearts Book 4):
JanThompson.com/tell

PILAR SANTIAGO IS IN NEVER A HOSTAGE:

This romantic suspense novel featuring Private Investigator Pilar Santiago is coming soon. Sign up for my mailing list to be notified when *Never a Hostage* (Defender Sweethearts Book 2) is published. Yes, I also write Christian romantic suspense and thrillers in addition to beach romances.

Subscribe to Jan's book news:
JanThompson.com/newsletter

RUBY TANAKA IS IN ALWAYS A MAVERICK:

FBI Special Agent Ruby Tanaka's story comes after Pilar's story in their own series. These novels are coming soon. To be notified when *Always a Maverick* (Defender Sweethearts Book 4) is published, be sure to sign up for my mailing list. Meanwhile, check out what's already published in this series.

Defender Sweethearts
JanThompson.com/defender

STELLA EVANS IS IN ZERO SUM:

In *Look for Me*, FBI Special Agent Stella Evans also makes an appearance. This busy agent then goes to Atlanta in her own book, *Zero Sum*, to track down the last hacker who is in trouble for working with a terrorist organization.

Zero Sum (Binary Hackers Book 1):
JanThompson.com/zerosum

Would you like to read a free ebook? A Christian beach romance novel, Ask You Later is the story of artist Leon Watts, who returns to Tybee Island and Savannah to jump-start his fledgling career, and meets a non-artistic art gallery director getting in his way. This prequel novel is a part of the Savannah Sweethearts collection, the series that comes before Vacation Sweethearts.

Download this FREE novel now:
JanThompson.com/ask-vacation

THE NEXT NOVEL IS PRAY FOR ME

VACATION SWEETHEARTS BOOK 5

When his ex-fiancée marries someone else, accountant-turned-landscaper Gus takes a vacation away from his Nassau home, visits his cousin in the USA, and falls in love with a pastor's daughter. Is it just romance on the rebound? Or is there something serious going on in this friends-to-more travel romance?

Pray for Me is the fifth novel in *USA Today* bestselling author Jan Thompson's Vacation Sweethearts series of standalone Christian travel romances. We first met Gus in *Smile for Me* (Vacation Sweethearts Book 1). At that time, he had left the corporate world and was a landscape gardener in the Bahamas. *Pray for Me* is his story.

UNWANTED TIME OFF…

After losing Veronique to another man, Augustus "Gus" Moss III needs a distraction and a change of scenery. He takes a leave of absence from his landscaping job in Nassau and flies to Atlanta, Georgia, to visit his cousin, Byron Moss. When Byron's whole family catches a cold, Gus ends up staying at Pastor Fitzpatrick's house, and finds himself drafted into serving in some of Midtown Chapel's summer ministries. He agrees to help because he is a friend of the pastor's eldest daughter, who seems to believe strongly in charity work.

UNEXPECTED MOMENTS…

Women's Ministry Director Tallulah "Tally" Fitzpatrick is busy ministering to women at conferences, and building a village of tiny homes for single mothers. Pulled in multiple directions, she is grateful to have Gus nearby—a steady friend who is around at just the right place and time. Although she has made up her mind to only marry an ordained pastor, she can't help being drawn to Gus, the landscaper with an accounting background and an MBA in finance.

UNAVOIDABLE CROSSROADS...

Are Gus and Tallulah just flirting with each other for the summer, or will the romance last into the winter of their lives? When the man of her dreams arrives in town, Tallulah has to choose between the two. Who will she let go? For sure, both Tallulah and Gus need a lot of prayer.

Pray for Me (Vacation Sweethearts Book 5):
JanThompson.com/pray

Vacation Sweethearts:
JanThompson.com/vacation

Subscribe to Jan's Mailing List for Book News:
JanThompson.com/newsletter

PRAY FOR ME CHAPTER 1 SNEAK PEEK

VACATION SWEETHEARTS BOOK 5

Letting go of Veronique was the hardest thing Gus had ever done in his life.

But let go, I must.

By the time Gus boarded his flight to go on a much-needed vacation, Veronique had been married for six months to another man and was now expecting her first child.

She had told him to forget her when they broke up a year ago, but Gus thought they might reconcile.

A baby with another man meant she had really moved on, didn't it?

So must Gus move on, or his name wasn't Augustus Isaac Moss III. It seemed that every Moss man had to endure heartache of some sort...

All except Gus's cousin Byron Moss.

What was Byron's secret to handling pain? Gus didn't think it had anything to do with Byron being an ordained pastor. He had been strong long before he entered the ministry, back when he was the assistant headmaster at the Chapel by the Sea Christian School in the Bahamas.

In the midst of his grief, Gus called Bryon to share his heart's sorrow.

Multiple phone calls later, Gus was still heartbroken.

When Byron invited Gus to visit him in Atlanta, Georgia, Gus jumped at the opportunity to get Veronique off his mind and out of his system. However, he was able to take only four weeks off due to the various work obligations he'd have to deal with as they approached the next semester.

The Chapel by the Sea Christian School in

Nassau was on summer break, and his landscaping crew could easily maintain the grounds without him for a month. They didn't need him. He'd be back in the Bahamas in June and back to work at the school before the teachers returned to campus in July.

Gus napped on the two-hour flight from Nassau's Lynden Pindling International Airport to Hartsfield-Jackson Atlanta International Airport, and woke up wondering what he would do in land-locked Atlanta. No beaches. No ocean. What kind of a place was that?

Exactly.

It would be different from his hometown, although he'd be arriving in late May, when the southern weather warmed up. At least the weather would remind him of home in Nassau.

Gus figured he could handle it. He closed his eyes as the flight attendants collected trash from the passengers on the short flight.

He recalled the Skype conversation he'd had with his cousin just the week before.

"You need a new project," Byron had said.

"A distraction?" Gus asked.

"Well, to reset—or realign—your focus back to God."

"How would a project do that?"

"You move on and you regroup. Recalibrate."

Gus laughed.

"What?" Byron asked.

"You might have left the Bahamas five years ago, but you're still the same Byron I know. Your thesaurus remains. Reset. Realign. Regroup. Recalibrate."

Byron looked amused. "I did that, didn't I?"

"You forgot one word."

"What?"

"Refocus."

"I used it as a noun."

"I supposed you sort of did, Professor Moss."

"Now I'm going to put on my counselor hat and recommend a change of scenery," Byron said. "If you can get away from work for a couple of months, Tina and I would love to have you stay at our house. There's plenty of volunteer work available at church if you want to keep busy and get your mind off you-know-who."

It had been a great idea until this morning, when Byron had texted to say that both his kids, Brielle and Myla, had come down with the flu, and pregnant Tina was catching it too, so would Gus mind staying at Pastor Daniel Fitzpatrick's house for a week until they all got over their sickness?

At first, Gus almost canceled his plans. He could always fly to Atlanta a couple of weeks later when everyone was well. Then his sense of curiosity got the better of him. When he'd visited Byron and Tina a year before, his friend Tally had introduced him to her parents, Pastor Fizz—as they all called him—and Riona, his wife of fifty years. Perhaps they could advise Gus on what constituted a successful marriage, although their three daughters were as yet unmarried, including the oldest one, Tally, who'd become a friend of his, albeit long distance.

Gus spoke to no one as he disembarked from the Boeing 737 and followed the crowd going down the hall and escalator toward the airport train. He could have walked the long way to baggage claim, but he didn't feel like it this afternoon. Besides, he had to get to the MARTA rapid transit for a ride to Midtown Chapel before Byron finished work for the day. They had planned to eat dinner together, just two cousins catching up on life. After that, Byron was supposed to drop Gus off at Pastor Fizz's house in Decatur somewhere.

An hour later, Gus found himself walking out of the MARTA train station at North Avenue, then crossing West Peachtree Street toward Midtown

Chapel at the corner of Spring Street and Ponce de Leon Avenue.

With a backpack on his back, he started to whistle "The Happy Wanderer," a campfire song he'd sung as a kid, back in his Boy Scout days. However, the Atlanta heat beat down on him, and his backpack stuck to his sweaty shoulder blades.

Of course, he had to choose the hottest day of the month to visit Atlanta. Eighty-eight degrees on the Fahrenheit scale was no joke.

He wiped sweat off his forehead and trudged on the sidewalk.

The city of Atlanta was huge and sprawling, but this side of town didn't have too many tall buildings. A couple of blocks away was the Fox Theatre, a favorite of Gus's aunt, Nancy. Perhaps the next time she came to town, Gus could take her there again so that she could enjoy the Möller organ, installed in 1929.

Of course, Byron could go too, since Aunt Nancy was his mother.

Since his own parents had passed away when he had been only a teenager, Gus was raised with his cousins by his aunt. These days, Gus was still close to Aunt Nancy. They talked business, even though Gus had left the white-collar field a long time ago. He had a feeling that Nancy had been trying to persuade him to get back into the family business and put his Harvard MBA to good use.

Instead, Gus had chosen to leave the corporate world behind and work as a landscaper and gardener at a small Christian school. He didn't want to return to long working hours and burnouts.

No thank you.

The short walk was easy for Gus. The sidewalk was empty except for a few people here and there. Everyone else seemed to be driving, and traffic was picking up both ways.

He wondered what all those people were doing out and about. He supposed that some were tourists like him.

Midtown Chapel took up a whole block. Once abandoned, the old nineteenth-century church building had almost been demolished. Pastor Fizz and his historian friends had come together to save the stained glass and pipe organ. They'd raised so much money that they were able to save the entire building and its surrounding grounds also.

Gus walked up to the front door. It was made of old oak wood from St. Simon's Island—from the same grove that had produced wood for the USS *Constitution* tall ship.

The metal knockers looked imposing.

Unfortunately, no one came to the door when Gus knocked.

He texted Byron. Byron texted back some instructions.

"Ah, yes. I knew that. I forgot." Gus pocketed his phone. "The staff door in the back."

He rounded the corner of the building and walked toward the staff parking lot. There were two church buses and several vehicles. A white van pulled up to a side door marked "Staff Only."

The driver's-side door opened, and a woman exited the van. She was wearing a bright tangerine T-shirt, a pair of cargo shorts, and hiking boots.

Gus almost didn't recognize her. She had cut her hair shorter than usual—above her shoulders— and was wearing sunglasses.

"Gus!" she said. "You made it here safely."

Tallulah Fitzpatrick.

Tally.

Gus barely nodded. Maybe he was mistaken. His friend had been as skinny as a twig several years ago, the first and last time he'd seen her in person. Last year, when Gus had visited Atlanta, she was out of town, speaking at a women's conference somewhere.

Today she was filled out in all the right places. Gus didn't know why he noticed that. And she was tanned, like someone who spent a lot of time outdoors.

She smiled that devastating smile that made everything okay, even if his heart still hurt from the recent loss.

"I thought that was you," Tally said.

"How are you doing?" Gus walked toward her and the glass door.

"Busy as ever. You?"

"Same." Actually, no. The first half of the year had been long and difficult. But he didn't have to tell everyone.

Tally stood by the glass door. "I'm guessing you're going inside."

Gus nodded. "I'm meeting Byron."

Before Tally could pull out her keycard, someone opened the door from the inside. It was Byron. And he was coughing.

"Uh-oh." Tally shook her head. "You too? It's going around."

"The only reason you're not getting it is that you haven't been in the building much this week." Byron coughed again.

"Since you're both able-bodied men, may I ask

you to help me carry some boxes from the storage room downstairs to the van?" Tally asked.

"Are you putting him to work right away?" Byron pointed to Gus. "He just flew in for a vacation. And I'm sick."

"Yes, but are your muscles sick too?" Tally looked concerned.

Gus removed the backpack from his back and stretched. "I don't mind. I need a glass of cold water first."

Tally walked back to her van, opened the cargo door, and retrieved a bottle of cold water from a red cooler.

Red, her favorite color. Gus remembered Tally wearing either a red skirt or a red blouse that September she was in Nassau several years ago. She'd spent more time ministering to the women and speaking at their women's retreat hosted at the Chapel by the Sea Christian School, where he worked, than she did walking around campus. He'd only chatted with her at their faculty and church staff dinners, when he wasn't busy with his land-scaping work.

Her red outfit and that smile were the two things that Gus hadn't forgotten about Tally.

"Thank you," Gus said.

Tally pointed to Gus's backpack. "That's all you brought?"

Gus nodded, wondering what she was getting at.

"I know you're staying at my parents' house tonight. I'm going there after I drop off the boxes at the warehouse. I could use some help unloading them. If you help me do that, I'll take you to my parents' place afterward."

Byron chuckled. "You're three steps ahead of us, Tally."

"How did you know where I'm staying?" Gus asked. "Other than the fact that Pastor Fizz is your dad?"

"Colette called me. Mom is trying to set her up with you." Tally laughed.

"I'm not interested in anyone." Gus tried not to look stunned that Riona Fitzpatrick was playing matchmaker again. He had heard of her reputation.

"It's too soon, I told her." Tally carried on like it was no big deal talking about a friend this way. "First, you have to get over your grief."

"Grief?" Gus drew a deep breath.

"Yep. Didn't you lose someone you thought you couldn't live without?"

"Ah..." Gus shouldn't have shared that much information with anyone, but who had he told? He certainly hadn't said much in their private group chat.

"My friend, 'grief' is the word." Tally patted his shoulder. "But you're still here. Alive and well. You survived. Don't worry. You'll get over it soon, with God's help."

"Thanks." Gus wanted to walk away and not talk about his private issues, but there was nowhere to go. Besides, he needed a ride to wherever he was staying.

Why couldn't he just stay at a hotel? Away from everyone?

"Everyone knows." Gus stared at Byron. "And here I am trying to get away."

"Not everyone," Tally answered for Byron. "Just his family and my family."

"They didn't hear it from me. I didn't say anything to anyone but Pastor Fizz." Byron lifted his palm in surrender.

"Your counseling pastor, no less." Gus kept his voice down.

"Dad has nothing to do with how we know. He doesn't tell anyone anything, not even Mom," Tally said. "You might have forgotten that Colette and Veronique's sister, Daniella, are best friends."

"They are?" Gus hadn't paid attention to Veronique's sister's friends.

"Yeah. Lots of friendships are made on those ministry trips that Midtown Chapel and Riverside Chapel do together at your church in Nassau." Tally glanced at Byron. "And marriages too."

Byron nodded, and coughed.

"You're sick," Tally said. "Go home, Byron."

She turned to Gus. "Seriously, don't worry. Don't be in a rush to get over it. Grief takes time, and it comes in stages. It took me five years to get over being left at the altar—in Hawaii, no less. But I got over it, with God's help and a lot of counseling from Dad. I'm happily single now, but the downside of that is I can't get help carrying supplies to the warehouse."

"Is that what a boyfriend is to you?" Gus tilted his head. "A porter?"

Tally patted his arm. "See? Humor is part of the healing process. You're on the way."

"On the way to where?" A third male voice said. The man came up behind Tally.

Gus didn't know who the man was, but he could see Tally's face change from cheery to annoyed. She drew a deep breath and turned around.

"You need any help?" the man asked.

"No. Thank you, Silas. I've got all the help I

need." Tally's voice was calm, indicating to Gus that she didn't feel threatened.

"I see two beta males." Silas flexed his large arms slightly. "I think you need me."

Gus didn't say a word. Neither did Byron, who was texting on his phone. Gus knew Byron well enough to know that he would defend himself. Perhaps this Silas dude was a known troublemaker and the best way to deal with him was to ignore his taunts.

Gus waited to see how Tally handled Silas. Perhaps he could take his cue from her.

Tally glanced at her watch. "You better hurry, Silas. If you're late again, my dad might not want to meet with you this late in the day anymore. It's past his usual office hours."

"Okay. See you." Silas ignored everyone else and made a beeline for the staff door, which was now locked.

Byron put away his phone and unlocked the door for Silas. "I'll walk you to Pastor Fizz's office."

Only Tally and Gus were left, standing outside in the afternoon sun.

"Is he a member of the church?" Gus asked.

"A visitor. I was hoping to be out of here before he arrived, but I was caught in traffic getting back from the warehouse, so my timing isn't good today."

"Is that the warehouse in Decatur?"

She raised an eyebrow. "You know about it?"

Gus nodded. "Byron told me it was an answer to prayer when someone paid for a year's use of it."

"We have way more donations than we have space."

"What kind of donations?"

"Since we started building those tiny homes as a part of our affordable housing ministry for single mothers, donations have poured in from all over the place."

"Sounds like a good ministry."

"Yep."

"What is it called?"

"Midtown Chapel Village," Tally said. "I had suggested we name it after our theme verse, James 1:27, the one that says, 'Pure and undefiled religion before God and the Father is this: to visit orphans and widows in their trouble, and to keep oneself unspotted from the world.' However, my women's ministry team decided that some of the single moms we're trying to reach might be turned off by something so declarative."

"Isn't being a Christian declarative as it is?"

"I know, right? But I got outvoted, so we settled on the idea of a village, a community, where the kids can feel safe."

"And you put the verse somewhere."

"Everywhere." She turned around to show the words on the back of her tangerine T-shirt.

"You're not wearing a red shirt," Gus blurted.

"Red?"

"You got outvoted again?"

"No, actually. We have T-shirts of many colors. I bought one of each and wear them in rotation." She stepped aside to reveal the side of the van. "Here's the verse again."

"James 1:27" was emblazoned on that side of the van in bold letters.

Tally smiled. "Want to put your backpack in the van? I'll lock it as we haul stuff out of the church."

"Good idea. Thanks."

Tally handed Gus another bottled water and a hand towel.

"What's this for?" Gus squeezed the hand towel.

"You're sweating bullets." She pointed to his forehead.

Gus didn't realize he was sweating. "It's a hot day."

The hand towel was soft and smelled of lavender. He gulped down the water.

"I apologize for the micro-plastic you're ingesting, but these were on sale, so I had to save ministry money."

Gus nodded. He was trying to get used to Tally's jokes. Then again, maybe she wasn't joking.

Tally locked the van. "Can't be too careful in Atlanta."

"Can't be too careful anywhere in the world these days," Gus said.

"I know, right? However, truth be told, I've forgotten to lock the vehicle door a couple of times, and nothing happened."

Gus nodded. "At the end of the day, only God can truly keep us safe."

He followed Tally into the church building. The air conditioner was still on at full blast even though it was past five o'clock, and most of the staffers had gone home on a slow Friday.

Tally took off her sunglasses, revealing light brown eyes. They were kind eyes, unlike Veronique's more intense ones.

"We're going to need a couple of carts. We can get them near the church kitchen." Tally led Gus down the hallway. "Thank you so much for helping me."

"No problem at all." And he meant it.

∾

Pray for Me (Vacation Sweethearts Book 5)
JanThompson.com/pray

Vacation Sweethearts
JanThompson.com/vacation

Jan Thompson's Book News Mailing List:
JanThompson.com/newsletter

ACKNOWLEDGEMENTS

Many thanks to my Georgia Press publishing team for keeping up with my writing schedule.

With God-given eyes for copyediting details, Lenda Selph is my patient proofreader extraordinaire. I appreciate her and thank God for her invaluable hard work.

I am grateful to God for my husband and son for their support and encouragement.

And I'll always remember my beloved mother and my late father for having instilled in me the love of reading and writing from a very early age. I miss my father here on earth, but I will see him in heaven some bright day.

Most of all, I am eternally thankful to my Lord and Savior, Jesus Christ, who died on the cross to save me from my sins and rose again from the grave to give me eternal life. Without Him, I can write and do nothing.

Jan Thompson
John 3:16

BOOKS BY JAN THOMPSON

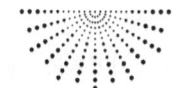

CHRISTIAN ROMANTIC SUSPENSE & BEACH ROMANCE

BINARY HACKERS (NEAR-FUTURE INSPIRATIONAL ROMANTIC THRILLERS)

- Book 1: Zero Sum
- Book 2: Zero Day
- Book 3: Zero Base
- Book 4: Zero Trust

PROTECTOR SWEETHEARTS (CHRISTIAN ROMANTIC SUSPENSE)

- Book 1: Once a Thief
- Book 2: Once a Hero

- Book 3: Once a Spy
- Book 4: Twice a Fighter
- Book 5: Twice a Convict
- Book 6: Twice a Soldier

DEFENDER SWEETHEARTS (CHRISTIAN ROMANTIC SUSPENSE)

- Book 1: Never a Traitor
- Book 2: Never a Hostage
- Book 3: Never a Fugitive
- Book 4: Always a Maverick
- Book 5: Always a Champion
- Book 6: Always a Guardian

SAVANNAH SWEETHEARTS (CHRISTIAN COASTAL CITY & BEACH TOWN ROMANCE)

- Prequel: Ask You Later
- Book 1: Know You More
- Book 2: Tell You Soon (Romance with Suspense)
- Book 3: Draw You Near
- Book 4: Cherish You So
- Book 5: Walk You There

- Book 6: Love You Always (Romance with Suspense)
- Book 7: Kiss You Now
- Book 8: Find You Again
- Book 9: Wish You Joy (Christmas Year Round)
- Book 10: Call You Home

VACATION SWEETHEARTS (CHRISTIAN TRAVEL ROMANCE)

- Book 1: Smile for Me
- Book 2: Reach for Me (Romance with Suspense)
- Book 3: Wait for Me (Romance with Suspense)
- Book 4: Look for Me (Romance with Suspense)
- Book 5: Pray for Me
- Book 6: Care for Me
- Book 7: Cheer for Me

SEASIDE CHAPEL (CHRISTIAN SMALL TOWN BEACH ROMANCE)

- Book 1: His Longing Heart (second edition of Share with Me)
- Book 2: His Wake-Up Call (second edition of Step with Me)
- Book 3: His Morning Kiss (previously published as Sing with Me)
- Book 4: His Quiet Serenade
- Book 5: His Waiting Love
- Book 6: His Beach Retreat

Subscribe to Jan Thompson's mailing list: JanThompson.com/newsletter

SEASIDE CHAPEL

Welcome to *USA Today* bestselling author Jan Thompson's Seaside Chapel Christian beach romance series. These novels are set on real-life St. Simon's Island, Georgia—a beach town where history is all around and the future is a moment away—and the neighboring fictitious Seaside Island, where the rich and famous live.

Savor the small-town atmosphere and the warm southern beaches of St. Simon's Island and the idyllic Golden Isles along the Atlantic Ocean. Enjoy the music of the orchestra and hymns of the church, and hang out with our Christian friends who attend Seaside Chapel, a little church by the sea known for its beach weddings and fair share of love and life.

As these Christians grow in their knowledge and understanding of God, they are tested in their spiritual maturity, their love lives, and their relationships with others. Share their heartaches and healing, and cheer them on as they celebrate faith, family, and friends.

JanThompson.com/seaside

- Book 1: His Longing Heart (second edition of Share with Me)
- Book 2: His Wake-Up Call (second edition of Step with Me)
- Book 3: His Morning Kiss (previously published as Sing with Me)
- Book 4: His Quiet Serenade
- Book 5: His Waiting Love
- Book 6: His Beach Retreat

SAVANNAH SWEETHEARTS

Welcome to the new south! From *USA Today* bestselling author Jan Thompson come these clean and wholesome, sweet and inspirational Christian romances set on the romantic beaches of Tybee Island and in the coastal town of Savannah, Georgia.

Meet a group of multiracial and multiethnic churchgoing Christians who love the Lord, work hard in their careers, and seek God's will for their love lives. Against a backdrop of ocean, sand, and sun, these inspirational romances showcase aspects of the human need for God and for one another. Have some tea, settle in a comfortable reading chair, and enjoy these sweet celebrations of faith, hope, and love in Jesus Christ.

JanThompson.com/savannah

- Prequel: Ask You Later
- Book 1: Know You More
- Book 2: Tell You Soon (Romance with Suspense)
- Book 3: Draw You Near
- Book 4: Cherish You So
- Book 5: Walk You There
- Book 6: Love You Always (Romance with Suspense)
- Book 7: Kiss You Now
- Book 8: Find You Again
- Book 9: Wish You Joy (Christmas Year Round)
- Book 10: Call You Home

VACATION SWEETHEARTS

Travel with our friends from Savannah, Georgia, to the coast and to the mountains. Cheer them on as they celebrate the immeasurable grace and undeserved mercy of God through Jesus Christ.

The Vacation Sweethearts novels are a spin-off of Jan's Savannah Sweethearts series, and fans will recognize familiar faces from Riverside Chapel, a church in the coastal city of Savannah, Georgia. In fact, we might even visit the beach town of Tybee Island from time to time to visit old friends and beloved families...

JanThompson.com/vacation

- Book 0 (Prequel): Time for Me
- Book 1: Smile for Me (International Romance)
- Book 2: Reach for Me (Romance with Suspense)
- Book 3: Wait for Me (Romance with Suspense)
- Book 4: Look for Me (Romance with Suspense)
- Book 5: Pray for Me (International Romance)
- Book 6: Care for Me
- Book 7: Cheer for Me (International Romance)

PROTECTOR SWEETHEARTS

Private investigator Helen Hu and her associates specialize in searching for missing persons and hunting for lost treasures. Join them in their adventure suspense around the world in *USA Today* bestselling author Jan Thompson's Protector Sweethearts, a series of Christian Romantic Suspense with a side of mystery. Protector Sweethearts is a spin-off of Savannah Sweethearts and Vacation Sweethearts.

JanThompson.com/protector

- Book 1: Once a Thief

- Book 2: Once a Hero
- Book 3: Once a Spy
- Book 4: Twice a Fighter
- Book 5: Twice a Convict
- Book 6: Twice a Soldier

DEFENDER SWEETHEARTS

Defender Sweethearts is a sister series to the Protector Sweethearts Christian romantic suspense collection. While the heroes in Protector Sweethearts search for lost treasures and lost people, the Defender Sweethearts novels focus on protecting the helpless and hopeless. The main characters in Defender Sweethearts come from the supporting cast in Protector Sweethearts.

JanThompson.com/defender

- Book 1: Never a Traitor

- Book 2: Never a Hostage
- Book 3: Never a Fugitive
- Book 4: Always a Maverick
- Book 5: Always a Champion
- Book 6: Always a Guardian

BINARY HACKERS

Like more suspense with your Christian romance? Like to read suspense thrillers? If you're looking for clean near-future romantic suspense without compromising the Christian faith, these books are for you.

From *USA Today* bestselling author Jan Thompson come these inspirational near-future cyberthrillers combining technothriller and romance, starting with Binary Hackers that feature computer specialists living at the edge of cyberspace, where they have to juggle being law-abiding truth-telling Christians while carrying out their assignments by any and all means possible.

The Binary Hackers series is set in the same story world as Jan's other books, and characters from the other series may make cameo appearances in this series and vice versa.

JanThompson.com/binary

- Book 1: Zero Sum
- Book 2: Zero Day
- Book 3: Zero Base

ABOUT JAN THOMPSON

USA Today bestselling author Jan Thompson writes clean and wholesome contemporary Christian romance with elements of women's fiction, Christian romantic suspense with an air of mystery, and inspirational international thrillers with threads of sweet Christian romance. Jan's books are for readers who love inspiring stories of faith, hope, and love in Jesus Christ.

Raised on a tropical island in the eastern hemisphere, Jan now lives and writes in the western hemisphere. Her international background gives her a unique multicultural and multiracial perspective to her novels and books. The island has never left her, and she reminisces about beach life in her beach romance novels.

When Jan is not busy writing small-town stories, she writes big-city romantic suspense and international technothrillers, a nod to her previous career in computer science. She weaves technology with human interests, reflecting the current and future digital world. And romance. There's always romance.

Beyond the printed page, Jan is a wife, mother, family scribe, avid reader, occasional artist, erstwhile pianist, and chief of staff to the family cat.

For God so loved the world
that He gave His only begotten Son,
that whoever believes in Him
should not perish but have everlasting life.

—John 3:16

www.ingramcontent.com/pod-product-compliance
Lightning Source LLC
Chambersburg PA
CBHW020214260626
47156CB00002B/373